KLC

D0064763

The
Monk
Upstairs

The Monk Upstairs

A Novel

Tim Farrington

HarperSanFrancisco
A Division of HarperCollins*Publishers*

THE MONK UPSTAIRS: *A Novel.* Copyright © 2007 by Tim Farrington. All rights reserved. Printed in the United States of America. No part of this book may be used or reproduced in any manner whatsoever without written permission except in the case of brief quotations embodied in critical articles and reviews. For information address HarperCollins Publishers, 10 East 53rd Street, New York, NY 10022.

HarperCollins books may be purchased for educational, business, or sales promotional use. For information please write: Special Markets Department, HarperCollins Publishers, 10 East 53rd Street, New York, NY 10022.

HarperCollins Web site: http://www.harpercollins.com
HarperCollins®, ✦®, and HarperSanFrancisco™ are
trademarks of HarperCollins Publishers.

FIRST EDITION
Designed by Joseph Rutt

Library of Congress Cataloging-in-Publication Data
Farrington, Tim
The monk upstairs : a novel / Tim Farrington — 1st ed.
p. cm.
ISBN: 978–0–06–081516–5
1. Single mothers—Fiction. 2. Bolinas (Calif.)—Fiction. 3. Landlord and tenant—Fiction. 4. Ex-monks—Fiction. I. Title
Ps3556.A775M67   2007
813'.54—dc22   2006041293

07 08 09 10 11 RRD (H) 10 9 8 7 6 5 4 3 2 1

But what mystery there lay
in "The Word was made Flesh,"
I could not even imagine.

—Augustine, *Confessions*

for Laurie Fox
beloved comrade

Chapter One

Thy vows are upon me, O God: I will render praises unto Thee.
Thou hast delivered my soul from death:
wilt Thou not deliver my feet from falling,
that I may walk before God in the land of the living?

PSALM 56

It was seven minutes past the appointed hour, and the bride-groom was nowhere to be found. Everyone was trying to put a good face on it, but a certain tension was inevitable. The organist, an ancient monk with a round pink face like a dried pomegranate, was muscling through another round of "On Eagle's Wings." Apparently his repertoire was limited; but the music took on an unsettlingly dirgelike quality the second time through. The guests sat quietly, their small talk long since expended, glancing discreetly at their watches, reading through their programs again as if they might have missed something. Chelsea Burke's baby had begun to cry, in one of the back pews, and the noise was approaching crisis proportions. Abbot Hackley, who was to perform the ceremony, stood at the front of the chapel with his hands folded in front of him, his heavy white chasuble trimmed with dazzling gold, a benediction waiting to happen. The look on his face was determinedly serene and seemed to suggest that this was all in God's plan, but from time to time he would sway a little, as if in a wind. The poor man was in the middle of the third course of some particularly savage clinical trial treatment for colon cancer, and the wedding had been scheduled to avoid the worst of his debilitation post-chemotherapy.

Peering through the crack in the door at the back of the chapel, Rebecca reviewed the major decisions of her life and decided that it had been a bizarre lapse of judgment to get married at all, much less at Mike's old monastery. They should have just eloped if they were going to take this mad leap. She had actually, seriously, truly in her heart wanted to do that, to jump in a car and drive up to Lake Tahoe. They could have gotten the damned thing done in some roadside chapel, had a few margaritas and some Mexican food, and been home before anyone was the wiser. But she'd made the mistake of mentioning the plan to her mother, and Phoebe had swung into panicked action and taken charge of constructing a more or less traditional fiasco.

Which was now duly unfolding. Rebecca turned to her mother and said, "I *told* you—"

"Don't even start," Phoebe said. She sat placidly on a folding chair someone had dug up for her, with the walker she'd been using during her recovery from the stroke she'd had the year before parked beside her. When the time came to process into the church, Phoebe had insisted, she was going to do it without the prop. Rebecca wasn't sure her mother could walk that far unsupported, and the image of Phoebe sprawled halfway up the aisle like a beached fish was not helping her stress level. But there had never been any stopping Phoebe.

"He'll show," Bonnie said. She was the maid of honor; it was her duty to be upbeat. And Bonnie could afford to be generous: her own wedding at Grace Cathedral the previous autumn had gone like extravagant clockwork. "His watch is probably off. Did you make sure he'd reset it at the switch from daylight savings time?"

"That was weeks ago. Surely we'd have known by now if he was running an hour behind the rest of the world." But even as she said it, Rebecca realized that it might not be so. Mike was often enough several hundred years, if not millennia, out of sync with the rest of the world, and he was perfectly capable of losing the stray hour here or there, like a pair of socks kicked under the bed of eternity.

"He's out there praying, or whatever it is he does," Bonnie insisted. "Or having a drink for the road."

"He'll show," Phoebe seconded. "Just relax, sweetheart. The man's a goner."

"If he needs to pray or drink at this point, we shouldn't be doing this," Rebecca said, but she was surrounded by resolute Pollyannas, and she took a deep breath. It was, clearly, a moment to simply exercise her inner resources and cultivate serenity. To Zen out, as Phoebe liked to say. Unfortunately, all that came to mind in terms of spiritual substance was the five Kübler-Ross stages of grief: denial, anger, bargaining, depression, acceptance. Rebecca had been cruising along in what she thought was acceptance until five minutes ago; but apparently that had just been denial, because she was seething now, in the old familiar way. It felt like she had spent most of her adult life in stage two of grief over her relationships with men.

The back door swung open, and Rebecca's heart leaped instantly into the purest stage five, without transition, but it was her daughter and her ex-husband, who had slipped out to look for Mike. And, it was clear at once, not found him. Mary Martha, looking a bit flushed in her pink flower girl dress with its even pinker ruffled front and puffy sleeves, had an air of uneasy compliance with circumstances beyond her grasp, like a dog on the way to the vet's. Rory looked the way he always looked when he had managed to escape a social gathering for a while, like he had just had two hits of something in the bathroom. He was wearing his only suit, the blue off-the-rack thing he kept on a hook for court appearances.

"No sign of him," he informed Rebecca, trying to look appropriately downcast and managing to keep it short of gleeful. But she couldn't begrudge him a little legitimate *schadenfreude*. No one wanted their ex's wedding to go perfectly; it was too much to expect of a human being.

"He'll show," Phoebe said.

"Has anyone tried his cell phone?" Mary Martha asked.

Everyone chuckled indulgently, it was so cute and precocious and postmodern, and then they all reached simultaneously for their phones because it was actually a great idea. Mike had resisted getting a phone for quite a while, but the dance of urban coordinations centering on Mary Martha being in first grade had eventually broken him down.

Bonnie, with her phone stashed for instant access in a nifty white satin dress-up purse the length of a tampon and the width of a pack of KitKats, won the race to get the number dialed. They all waited hopefully, but after a moment she shook her head and said, "No signal out here."

It made sense, unfortunately. The Bethanite monastery that had been Mike's home for twenty years was so far out in the second-growth redwood forest on the coast of Mendocino County that it always seemed like a surprise that they had running water. They still did the books by hand out here, the nearest paved road was six miles away, and the monks used the place's single computer mostly for playing blackjack.

Rebecca peeked through the door into the chapel again. Chelsea Burke had quieted her baby by opening her blouse and beginning to breast-feed. The monks sitting near her were all looking straight ahead toward the altar and had taken on an air of rapt absorption, as if they were listening to faint tendrils of angel song.

"He'll show," Rory said generously.

That did it. Rebecca thought of her wedding day with Rory, of waiting on the beach, four months pregnant with Mary

Martha, surrounded by a handful of stoned hippies, her horrified mother, and a minister of the Church of the Perfect Wave who had gotten his certificate through a correspondence course, while Rory bobbed beyond the breakers on his surfboard. If it hadn't been a little choppy that day, Rebecca had always suspected, he might not have come ashore at all. Rory's wet suit was still dripping when they finally got around to the ceremony, and his lips had been blue from the cold for their first conjugal kiss. It felt like marrying a seal. Rebecca had hoped for a different ceremonial spin, this second time around.

"I'm going to go find him," she announced now, and she started for the door in don't-mess-with-me fashion. Everyone hesitated, uneasy with the move, then leaned back to let her by. They'd all seen her lose it before, at one time or another, and God knew it wasn't pretty.

She felt better the moment she was outside. The May afternoon was chilly beneath a low, thick sky, and her bare arms rose at once into goose bumps. Mike had assured her that late spring was a glorious time in the monastery's woods, and in fact it had been clear for about twenty minutes just before noon, but the balance between land and sea had already tilted back toward the cool air streaming off the Humboldt Current, and threads of incoming mist wove through the upper branches of the tan oaks, firs, and redwoods, muffling the greens into funereal gray. It was probably a warm, clear day in the low eighties a couple of miles inland, but it was way too late to get married somewhere sunny, secular, and sane.

Rebecca skirted the jumble of cars in the muddy clearing serving as the monastery's makeshift parking lot. Ahead and to her right was the main complex of Our Lady of Bethany. Rebecca went first to the refectory where the monks took their silent meals, on the off chance that Mike was in there washing the lunch dishes or something. He was prone to such obscurities of menial service, and she knew that washing dishes always calmed him down. But the only one in the kitchen was a fresh-faced novice in an apron with "Taste and see that the Lord is good" written on it, who was laying out a tray of some kind of neo-Benedictine hors d'oeuvres for the reception. Rebecca saw a young Mike in him for a moment: the shaved head, the air of sturdy resignation and determined cheerfulness, and the heartbreaking innocence.

"Have you seen my bridegroom anywhere?" she asked.

The kid shook his head. He seemed distressed by the breakdown of the sacred routine and was clearly groping for something spiritual to say, but Rebecca had no time for it. She grabbed one of the bottles of Dom Pérignon that were stuck into one of the monastery's washtubs of ice like beer cans at a picnic, gave the startled young monk a wink in lieu of further clarification, and breezed out.

On the muddy driveway again she paused, the champagne bottle dripping on her off-white satin sling-backs. To her immediate right lay the dormlike residence buildings, the slapdash office, and the cute little misplaced abbatial chalet, crammed now with the rented medical paraphernalia of Abbot Hackley's prolonged demise. Beyond that were the monastery's gardens and its foggy peach orchard and artichoke patch. Men had been disappearing into this place since the monastery had been founded near the turn of the century by three peevish hermits seceding from the Cistercians; whole lifetimes of devotion had circled the holy drain and vanished into its depths, and it offered no end of nooks, niches, and refuge for those inclined to renounce the world of weddings and other mundane complexities. But Rebecca knew her man. Mike had found even the monastery's contemplative retreats inadequate, in the long run, and she took the barely discernible trail to the left, deeper into the forest.

W*hat time I am afraid, I will trust in Thee.*

There were two ways in, through fire and through water, and he turned into the fire, having learned by now in every nerve ending that the water's oasis was a mirage, a comfort that bloated, rotted, and stank; that the only peace, the unimaginable freedom, lay at the heart of the flame, after every oasis had dried up and every seeking after comfort had burned away. It was the precise opposite of what any child learned, touching a hot stove, but it was no trick. It was a thing your bones came to know, a thing burned into you by time and suffering. And this was prayer.

I indeed baptize you with water unto repentance; but he that cometh after me shall baptize you with the Holy Ghost, and with fire.

Mike sat on the floor in the middle of the shack, legs crossed, with only a scrap of dirty white prayer mat woven from thick strands of raw wool, a gift from a visiting Shaivite monk some twenty years ago, between him and the concrete floor. There was a prie-dieu with a wooden kneeler built into the east wall, below the shelf shrine to St. Martha, Our Lady of Bethany, but Mike had never used the thing. Neither, though, had he ever bothered to dispel anyone's impression that he did. His early contemplative experiences had come as a teenager, among Zen Buddhists, and he'd always found the basic cross-legged position best. But he'd had to fight so hard to get this sanctuary built at all that he hadn't wanted to push his luck by revealing his preference for a posture that might be interpreted as pagan.

It was strange to be here, back in the center of this rough floor, with the fog seeping in as coolness from every edge and corner of the shack, bearing witness to the thing's unlikely and haphazard construction. Strangest of all, perhaps, was how easy and true it felt, how much it seemed, sinking into this simple presence, that he had never left, that this was the reality and that all the adventures, the drama, dilemmas, and bafflement in the year between sittings here, had been the drifting of a forgetful instant, a hazy space-out between the moment of remembrance and the moment of return.

Mike had proposed the idea for the hermitage to Abbot Hackley a year and a half after he'd come to Our Lady of Bethany, believing it at the time to be a slam dunk: a prayer retreat, after all, at a monastery. The activity of building itself seemed another selling point: a sweaty project, calluses and holy blisters, exertion and tangible results. His abbot was relentless in his sense that Mike gave entirely too little energy to robust service. But Hackley had seen it differently, had smelled at once a failure of humility, the stink of holy ambition. And defiance, the incapacity to submit to the discipline of obedience.

True enough, Mike thought, looking back. He'd definitely wanted too much, at every step of his journey, but in the long run that too-muchness was a greed that only God could really cure. And as for the defiance . . . He'd paid dearly enough for that. The fights with Hackley had blocked out the horizon of his prayer life for years. Mike suspected it had been as much a catastrophe of ego and distraction of the soul for the abbot as it had been for him. But once the battle had been joined, it went on and on, mostly because neither man was willing to lose. So much for the contemplative community as a peaceful incubator of the love of God, a garden of serene devotion: the monastery was the world in small, petty, prickly, and in your face. To be in it but not of it was still the impossible goal. You realized that at some point and got on with it.

They'd cut a deal of sorts eventually: Mike could build the shack, but it had to be done in his free time and with scrap materials only, nothing that could be used for anything else. Since there really *was* no free time in the round of the monastic hours, and precious little went to waste in Our Lady of Bethany's frugal economy, where they were all by strict design *pauperes cum paupere Christo,* poor men sharing the poverty of Christ, the abbot had no doubt believed the conditions sufficiently impracticable to allow Mike to knock himself out, while Mike had just been glad to get to work.

The new refectory was being built at that time, and Mike had taken to rummaging in the dumpster beside the construction site at two in the morning, in the still hour before the community chanted vigils. As he seldom found any scraps larger than about twenty-three inches, he'd used the chunks of leftover board like bricks. Aside from the obvious, that Mike could build only in the dark, in forty-five-minute eruptions of insomnia flanked by prayer and prayer, the limit on the pace of construction at that point had been the nails: he'd gotten amazingly good at finding bent discards amid the sawdust and the mud and straightening them by candlelight, though his left thumbnail was soon perpetually black and his hands battered from hammer blows delivered in the dark.

For some time, the shack's walls had eased upward overnight in semisedimentary fashion, like an accumulation of wooden dew, an inch and a half at a time. But Mike had lost ten pounds in the first month, and his eyes sank back behind soggy bags of black, like bruises. He started falling asleep during the communal mass, and during the daily self-examination of faults against the Rule his dogged confessions of pride eventually began to draw smirks from the other monks. He was a walking lesson in spiritual hubris. The rainy season was coming by then, and the project more than ever seemed utterly quixotic. Abbot Hackley, meanwhile, continued to be serenely tolerant of Mike's exertions, apparently feeling the work to be essentially penitential, if not Sisyphean.

The turning point had come when the construction crew realized what was going on. For some reason Mike's struggle caught their imaginations, an underdog thing, perhaps, and suddenly a much higher quality of materials began to appear, mysteriously, in and around the dumpster: actual two-by-fours, whole boards consigned to the scrap pile for dubious degrees of warping, bags of nails with the merest tinge of rust, an entire piece of plywood someone had used for a sign, and another sheet that had been used as a walkway. Just when the shack's frame was finally up, a skeleton without much hope of a skin, half a roll of battered but viable tar paper got thrown away; several sheets of flashing and a slightly damaged tube of sealant appeared at a crucial moment in the roofing.

It all took place quietly, invisibly, under cover of darkness and silence, and by the time Abbot Hackley even realized he was losing, the fight was almost over. To add insult to injury, on the day the cement truck came to pour the final flooring of the new refectory, Mike was summoned from the monastery's silent lunch by one of the workers "to help them find a place to dispose of the extra concrete." He'd conceded that he had a place to dump it, and they'd backed the massive truck as far as possible into the woods and used a wheelbarrow for the last stretch of trail, hauling just enough cement for the shack's rough floor. The crew had poured out the gray stuff cheerfully, shared a cigarette with Mike and given him a wink, and driven off. Mike had been called back to his own monastic duties before he'd been able to fully level the floor, and even now, twenty years later, you could set a marble in the northeast corner and watch it slowly wander southwest, to bump at last against the far wall. But the thing was done.

Mike had knocked together the prie-dieu the next morning, having saved up a chunk of unblemished two-by-six. He'd never knelt on it himself, but in the years since then, the kneeler had come into its own: two distinct impressions were hollowed into the unpadded board, the knee shapes, decades deep now, of several generations of other monks. Despite its problematic history, the renegade prayer shack had quietly become an integral part of the monastery's life. For some years now, you'd even had to sign up in advance, particularly during Lent, for time in what had come to be called, formally, the Retreat House, though the old-timers still called it Brother Jerome's hut, if Abbot Hackley was not around. There had even been talk recently of rebuilding the structure, of making a proper chapel here, with a consecrated altar, a side cell, sink, and toilet, running water, possibly even electricity: a pious haven of stone stability. Mike hoped this would not happen. As it was, the hut felt just right: flimsy, isolated, almost furtive, a place to pray truly, a theft of time from a greedy world. A place where prayer still felt like what it really was, something dangerous.

Is not my Word like a fire? saith the Lord; and like a hammer that breaketh the rock in pieces?

He had drifted; you always drifted. Mike found his breath and rode it into the flame again, and memory sweltered and cracked in that soft fire, into shards of regret and bewilderment, benediction and dread: the mystery, the burning knot, the impossibility of self and world. The slipshod walls of scrap and junk sighed and settled like a hearth; the fear within him burned and burned, and he sat at the heart of the fire it fed and breathed cool air. It was his wedding day, and then it was any day; it was nothing, and then it was forever.

Chapter Two

If anyone wishes to become a disciple of mine,
let them take up their cross and follow me.

MATTHEW 16:23

Rebecca had a bad few minutes, thinking she might have gone down the wrong path, but at last she rounded a bend and spotted the odd little hut that Mike called the prayer shack. She'd heard the story of the thing's contested construction a couple of times by now, and she still had a hard time understanding what the fuss had been about. The shack was a harmless peculiarity, a whim. It looked like a kid's tree house that had fallen out of its tree, or the junk sculpture of a mad beachcomber.

Beyond a creek still swollen with late winter rains, the trail turned muddy for the last stretch, and Rebecca stopped at the edge of the water and considered the soggy passage with dismay. She was getting angry, disgusted with Mike and his holy extremities. She really wasn't dressed for all this muddy sacred ground, slogging up a redwood-forested Sinai, through manzanita bushes ablaze with the voice of God. But that was her man. At some point there was nothing to do but take your shoes off and let the shrubbery burn.

She slipped off her sling-backs, drew up the hem of her dress with the hand that still clutched the champagne bottle, and splashed through the creek, feeling the shock of the cold water. She slogged up the muddy rise toward the shack, and as she cleared the brush she found Brother What's-His-Name, James, Mike's best buddy at the monastery, sitting quietly outside the entrance on the big boulder someone had hauled in at some point, a sort of Zen centerpiece to the shack's hapless little garden of stones and herbs. James might have been thirty, but he looked too young to drink. Too young to vote, too young to drive, even. But Mike said he read fluently in four dead languages and three live ones, that he was some kind of theological prodigy, and that he had a killer three-point shot and a way with altar flowers.

He was whittling something, Rebecca saw, a female figure. A Mary, maybe: the Virgin on a stick. They sold the things in the monastery's gift shop. Sometimes James made whistles out of them. She'd bought one for Mary Martha the day before and then had to take it away because her daughter couldn't stop blowing on it and driving everyone crazy. The wooden sculpting was exquisite, but the details were so fine, and James's pocket-knife's blade so crude, that Rebecca wondered how he did it without cutting his hands. It looked dangerous to her.

The kid looked up as Rebecca approached, his face a study in sudden dismay, like a teenager caught smoking.

"Busted," Rebecca said.

"He said he'd be right out," James assured her hastily, speaking in that pointedly lowered tone characteristic of so many of the monastery's exchanges. A perpetual *shush,* as if Our Lady of Bethany were a librarian. Rebecca had been here less than twenty-four hours, and it was already starting to drive her a little nuts. You couldn't ask someone where the bathroom was in this place without disturbing somebody at their prayer. When these maniacs were talking at all.

"How long ago did he say *that?*"

Brother James just smiled, a trace of mystical smugness: God's time was not the time of human beings. Rebecca considered hitting him with the champagne bottle, then conceded the delay by setting her shoes on the boulder beside him.

"I'm sure he'll be out in a minute," James said amiably.

"Sixty seconds," Rebecca agreed, mirroring his tone. "And then I'm going in there and getting him."

Brother James looked alarmed. He'd meant a God-minute, of course: the divine margin for error. But she was twenty human minutes late for her own damned wedding. Rebecca said steadily, "Fifty-nine ... fifty-eight ... "

"I love your dress," James offered.

"Thank you. Fifty-six ... "

James gave up and returned to his carving. Rebecca watched an even strip curl away along the Virgin's belly, lifting discreetly toward the end, shaping the holy breast. The forest around them was silent in that distinct way redwood groves had, a churchlike stillness. The drooping, primeval ferns dripped audibly, and she could hear the stream. It felt a million miles away from everything. Mike said there were even spotted owls back here, in groves that had never been logged. Georgia-Pacific wanted to cut the whole mountainside down, had offered huge sums repeatedly. But the monks hadn't sold out yet. Mike had told her that hardly any of them cared about the owls, they just didn't want all that noise.

"Forty-five ...," Rebecca said. "Forty-four ... "

Brother James carved on. He had a quality that Mike had, the ability to serenely confound the most fundamental social expectations, to be silent in situations where most people would have felt the need to talk as strongly as the need to breathe. He was still working on the breast, was about half a shaving shy of the erotic, holding that fine line. Rebecca had an urge to startle him somehow, perversely, to see if the knife would dip too deep and sharpen the figure into carnality. Though she actually suspected that James was gay. His carvings of Jesus were exquisitely buff, managing to both venerate the reality of Incarnation and gently suggest that our Savior might work out at a gym in the Castro. She'd asked Mike about it the night before, and he'd shrugged and said he wasn't sure, that it would likely be years, if not decades, before James really dealt with his sexuality. But: probably.

Probably, my ass, Rebecca thought now. She said, "*Ten* ... "

"Nyuhn-uh," Brother James said, a perfect kid's inflection, exactly the way Mary Martha would have said it.

Rebecca laughed. "Nyuhn-*huh*," she said. "Nine ... eight ... seven, six, five four threetwo*one*."

Brother James stood up. Agreeably enough, a good loser. "Shall I go back and tell everyone you two will be along soon?"

"If anyone's still there."

"It's actually sort of hard to get out of this place," James said. He closed his pocketknife and slipped it, with the carving, into a deep pocket somewhere in his robe. It was amazing to Rebecca how much stuff some of these monks carried with them, invisibly, lost in those deep brown folds. Keys, hymnals, reading glasses, pens, screwdrivers, rosaries. They were like holy kangaroos.

She waited until James was out of sight, then stood up herself. She'd half-hoped Mike would respond telepathically to her presence; it would have been very romantic, in its way, if he'd appeared at the door just now, refreshed by the mystery of communion and primed by prayer to exchange their vows in an atmosphere of consecrated serenity. But apparently she was going to have to bust in on him after all.

The door was plywood, not a single sheet but three separate scraps, barely coherent, like pieces from different puzzles made to fit. It hung at a slightly drunken angle, and she could smell incense leaking around the edges, the Nag Champa Mike loved to burn. Rebecca put one hand on the door, carefully, to avoid splinters, and pushed. The thing stuck, and she pushed again, more firmly. The rack of wood swung grudgingly inward, more of a flop than a swing, and she stepped inside to meet her bridegroom.

• • •

The door slapped shut behind her at once on its own gravity—it was probably harder to get out of this place than to get into it. The wooden thump sounded enormous in the silence, and Rebecca flinched, then thought, *Good, that'll wake him up.*

It took her eyes a moment to adjust to the hut's dim interior; Mike either hadn't had the resources for windows or just hadn't cared. The only light in the room came from the single votive candle burning on the altar shelf and the tiny orange glow of the incense stick. By the time Rebecca's eyes made the transition and she could make out his figure sitting on the floor in the middle of the space, Mike's own eyes were open and he was smiling at her, quite naturally, as if they'd been watching a football game together and she'd gone out to the kitchen for a moment and come back with beers.

"Isn't this bad luck or something?" he said.

Rebecca laughed in spite of herself. She had assumed early in the relationship that his prayer states, which she imagined to be quite deep without really understanding what that meant, were more dramatic things, trancelike ascents into transcendent bliss or sunken plunges into exotic ecstasies, requiring elaborate reentry. What was all the fuss about, otherwise? What else could have compelled him to leave the world for so many years, what else could have sustained him in that weird exile, except something potent and remarkable and spectacularly impervious to normality? But she'd learned soon enough that he was right there, immediately, without transition. However she came in when he was at prayer, loud or soft, delicate or crude, loving or angry, Mike opened his eyes, and there he was. As if, for all the world, he'd just been sitting there waiting for her. He smiled, and there she was too.

"Bad luck is missing your own damned wedding," Rebecca said. "This is simple sanity."

Mike unfolded his legs by way of reply, lifted his butt, and rolled up his prayer mat. He never got mad when she disturbed him at his prayer. But Rebecca had noted that he did move farther away, in the long run, quietly and relentlessly, like a cat looking for a better nap spot: early in their relationship he had meditated in bed, and then on a pillow in the corner of the bedroom, and finally in the living room. Lately, apparently finding even the most obscure corners of the downstairs insufficient, he had taken to praying in the attic.

Rebecca hoped he didn't ever get farther away than this. She wasn't sure how many more creeks she was willing to cross.

She stepped close and held out a hand to help him up. Mike took it, and she leaned back against his weight as he rose, then came back to vertical in his arms. She could smell his shaving cream, the cheap stuff, with a touch of aloe; she could smell his cheap balsam-and-honey shampoo. He had a perfectly normal head of beautiful black hair now, and he had sworn not to cut it short again.

"You smell good," Mike said.

"You smell good."

"We both smell good," he said. "Let's get married."

"Funny you should mention that ... "

He released her to blow out the candle, and the room went black. The damp darkness smelled of squirrel shit and tar paper, lightly overlaid with Nag Champa. Mike moved to the door and rummaged briefly for his shoes, then groped for the loop of cord that served as the door's handle. The door stuck, inevitably, but finally yielded with a scrape and a creak, and they walked outside together into the sweetness of daylight. Mike was already dressed for the event, at least, Rebecca noted now with some relief. He'd been out here meditating in the woods in a goddamned tuxedo.

Outside, Mike moved to the boulder and sat down on it to tie his shoes, then straightened and took out a pack of cigarettes. Rebecca hesitated then decided, what the hell, late was late, a few more minutes couldn't hurt.

"You chased James off?" Mike smiled.

"Like a rabbit," Rebecca said. He hadn't offered her a cigarette; he knew she was trying to quit. Mary Martha's first-grade education included large doses of vehement antismoking instruction; her daughter was now under the impression that it was just a matter of hours or days after lighting up that you would die. It was wonderful, in its way, but very inconvenient.

Mike took a drag and blew the smoke away from her, then turned and met her eyes.

"This is crazy," he said.

"I know," Rebecca said.

"No, I mean *really* crazy."

She recognized what he was offering: A time-out for the countermovement of sanity. A chance to recall their actual selves. It was one of Mike's best qualities, that willingness to step out of the traffic of the world, to ignore the honking horns, to find someplace amid the roadside trash to seek the moment's deeper reality. Rebecca had come to count on it in him. She just wasn't sure she could stand it right now. There were almost a hundred people sitting back in that ridiculous little chapel waiting for them to play the happy bride and groom, and try as she might, she just wasn't spiritual enough to ignore that.

Mike went on, "I had really pictured something less . . . *big*. Less—"

"Farcical?" Rebecca suggested, trying to hurry things along a bit.

"That seems harsh. But—yes. Less burlesque. Less over-the-top."

"I told you we should have gone to Tahoe. But you wanted to humor Phoebe."

"It seemed like simple decency at the time."

"Decency is never simple," Rebecca said. "You try to be decent, and one thing leads to another, and the next thing you know you're dressed like the little plastic couple on top of the wedding cake, trapped in costume on a mountaintop with all your friends and a bunch of guys in brown dresses."

"There's a back way down the mountain," Mike said. "You can follow the river to Fort Bragg. I know a bar in town where happy hour starts at three. I think we can still make it."

"What about the sacred reality of marriage?"

"If we can't find the sacred reality of marriage in the Typhoon during happy hour, I don't know where we're going to find it."

They were silent for a moment. Rebecca knew that she should be giving her full and undivided attention to this profound and timely discussion of the biggest commitment of their lives, but all she could think about at the moment was snatching the cigarette out of his hand. Just one puff, she thought. She could write it off to the crush of circumstance. To stress management. Surely even a first-grader could understand that.

"Is that champagne?" Mike asked.

Rebecca looked down at the bottle in her hand. She had forgotten all about it. "I grabbed it in the kitchen," she said. "I guess I wanted to have something handy to drown my sorrows, in case you had decided to bail." Mike was silent for such a long moment that she felt a jarring burst of electricity along every nerve in her body. "You're *not* bailing, are you?"

"No," he said. "There's a baby in this damned bathwater. I was just trying to think of another reason to open the bottle."

Rebecca laughed. She forgot: it was as simple as that. She just loved being with the guy. Possibly enough that not even their own wedding could screw it up.

"We really do need to get back before Abbot Hackley dies, Mike," she said, for the record.

"That old fart is going to live forever. He'll bury us all."

"When my mother starts giving me shit, I'm blaming you."

"Which is only as it should be."

That seemed to cover all the bases. Rebecca surrendered the bottle. As Mike tore away the foil, she plucked the cigarette from his lips and took a deep what-the-hell drag. Maybe the champagne would cover up the smell of smoke on her breath, she thought. With luck, her daughter might just think she was an alcoholic.

Mike worked at the cork with his thumbs until it blew out of the bottle's mouth. It arced wonderfully through the air and landed on the roof of the shack. They looked at each other and laughed.

"Think of some gung-ho young monk finding that in fifty years," Mike said. "Talk about your divine mysteries." He waited for the champagne to stop foaming over, then handed her the bottle.

"We might as well still be in high school," Rebecca said. "Jesus, thirty-eight years old, and I'm out here in the woods with my boyfriend, smoking cigarettes and drinking wine out of the bottle."

"You say that like it's a bad thing," Mike said.

She raised the champagne. "Here's to being late for our own wedding, sweetheart."

"And to decency."

"And to—uhhh—"

"The sacred reality of marriage."

"If we can stand it."

"Qui perfecte diligit, nupsit," Mike said.

"Amen, I think," Rebecca said, and drank.

She was glad for that wine, and for the time-out, twenty minutes later, watching Phoebe make her way up the aisle on the arm of Brother James. Her mother's progress was glacially slow without her walker, and the journey seemed to take forever. Rebecca thought that she might not have been able to stand it, would almost certainly have squandered the moment on fretting and anxiety, had she and Mike not been so incredibly rude and made everyone wait while they got themselves together a bit. But as it was, Rebecca's eyes stung with tears, because once you relaxed enough to see it, the dignity and splendor of Phoebe shuffling through the rose petals strewn a moment before by Mary Martha was one of the most beautiful things she had ever seen.

Beyond her mother, she could see Mike waiting at the altar, lovely in his unstrained patience; and Bonnie on the other side, with Mary Martha, and poor pale Abbot Hackley himself, seemingly propped upright by the stiff gold of his chasuble alone, all of them watching Phoebe with eyes full of exquisite and unhurried love.

And when Rebecca's turn came at last, and she followed her mother up the aisle, moving at her own stately pace along that laboriously cleared path through the rose petals, she felt those same eyes of love on her, and she felt unexpectedly buoyed and moved, borne along by that unforeseeable grace. She was glad that they had gone for decency after all, in the end. And even gladder, perhaps, that she was just drunk enough to appreciate it.

Chapter Three

God's foolishness is wiser than human wisdom,
and God's weakness is stronger than human strength.

1 CORINTHIANS 1:25

Phoebe had come to see the slowness as a blessing of sorts. Not that she had any choice. The slowness was just how it was now, it was what she moved in, like a new kind of weather, a variant kind of air, as viscous as half-set Jell-O. You could try to go fast in it, from habit and history and wishful thinking, and suffer immensities of frustration, or you could cut your speed losses and just see what the world was like now, to these slowed eyes and this slowed self. She'd been a speed person all her life, and the fight had not been pretty, but by now she'd pretty much gotten it. Slow was where it was at. It certainly brought out a different aspect of things.

She was practicing shoelace knots on her number two pair of sneakers. Her number one pair had Velcro instead of laces, and that had been amusing and even enjoyable while Mary Martha had Velcro sneakers too, but Mary Martha had recently made the leap to laced shoes, and Phoebe was determined to keep pace. Mary Martha actually knew two different bow-tying techniques, which she called the Bunny and the Rabbit; she could keep them separate in her head somehow, and she knew all the steps to each. She had been trying to teach them to Phoebe, which was delightful and very sweet but often a little confusing; and the truth was that despite a significant lead in the abstract, Mary Martha didn't really have either technique down yet herself. Phoebe kept hoping her own fingers would remember the skill somehow, but she'd had no luck so far. Her body remembered some things, her brain remembered others; but some things she was just having to relearn from scratch. And some things, she knew, were probably gone for good.

She made the bunny's ear, or maybe it was the rabbit's, she could never keep them straight, and chased the bunny around the garden and into the burrow and out the other side, but the bow fell apart for some reason, so maybe it had been the rabbit after all. She wished her granddaughter were there to help her. Mary Martha at least was clear about the mechanics of both techniques; it was her execution that was off.

She was starting again, a rabbit's ear this time, when a startling crash sounded upstairs, and then a second. It sounded like someone breaking through a wall. Rebecca and Mike were in Hawaii on their honeymoon, and Mary Martha was spending the week with Rory, so there shouldn't have been anyone up there, much less anyone who was apparently destroying the place with a sledgehammer.

Phoebe looked at her telephone, to which Rebecca had taped an index card with 911 written on it in big black numbers. She picked up the receiver and looked at the buttons. She had the concept of numbers down, she knew that the black things on the card matched things on the telephone buttons, and sometimes, maddeningly, capriciously, all the connections were abundantly clear, but this was not one of those times and it all looked somewhat Sumerian.

That was how things were now: she could remember the Sumerians, the rise of agricultural civilization in the Fertile Crescent, the origins of writing in hieroglyphs on clay tablets, but she couldn't dial 911 on a phone sitting in front of her. The nine was in the bottom row and the one was in the top row, but Phoebe didn't really want to start trying combinations at random. A long list of people's phone numbers was taped to the table beside the phone, but those all had at least seven numbers. She probably should have been a little more honest with Rebecca about her actual reading capacities, but Phoebe knew Rebecca would never have gone on her honeymoon then. So she'd bluffed.

And now life was calling her bluff. Oh, well, Phoebe thought, and reached for her cane. Her walker wouldn't get her up the stairs; if she was going to charge up there to confront the vandal, it would have to be at the snail's pace of her cane.

She wasn't sure what she was going to do when she got to the top, but she'd found since the stroke that things usually worked out, you just had to jump in without really knowing all the hows, and go at it on faith. Often it was clear by the time you got there, and when it was not, as with shoelaces, well, then you just dealt with it.

She lay on black sand, the newest sand on the planet, letting the sun soak into her. The warmth here seemed to have an intelligence of its own, unhurried, gentle, and penetrative, like the hands of a good masseuse; Rebecca could feel it finding its way into her, layer by layer, sinking through her skin to her muscles and organs, to her heart, and deeper, to somewhere that had been screaming for warmth for years.

It was disorienting—not that this miracle happened but that it seemed so natural. It was more like remembering than like making, more like a return than a journey. How was it possible to forget something as fundamental as the way the sun felt baking a moment into eternity in your flesh? The way that time turned into simplicity in such warmth. They were only a few hours west of their usual location on the same turning planet. You could stand on this shore at dawn and watch this healing sun come up from where they lived what they thought of as their real lives. It was the same ocean, and the same sky; but it was a different world. And yet it felt like a kind of coming home.

A honeymoon, Rebecca thought languidly, stretching her oiled legs and digging her toes into the sand. The thought was unlike her. She didn't actually *believe* in honeymoons. She was opposed to them on principle. Honeymoons were like the towel beneath her, a big new $5.99 tourist monstrosity of flaming

orange-red, the color of molten lava, that was going to look silly
as soon as they were back in cold, gray San Francisco. The cheap
cotton was so thin it felt like rarified cardboard, and it was more
or less useless as a towel, just moving the water around on your
skin without actually absorbing any of it. This vivid symbol of
their honeymoon happiness wouldn't get her dry after the first
Monday morning shower and certainly wouldn't survive more
than a run or two through the washing machine. The colors
would bleed, the edges would fray, and she'd have to go to K-
Mart and buy something fluffy and durable in good old Martha
Stewart navy blue.

And yet ... it was such a pretty thing, like a feather from a
dream bird.

Mike came trotting up from the water just then, and Rebecca
smiled just at the sight of him. It was still almost impossible to
think of him as her husband without giggling. It felt more like
they were kids, playing at marriage on the beach: here's the sand
castle that we live in, and here's the sand castle where we go to
work. This piece of wood is our car. Any minute now a wave
could come in and change the entire landscape of the game; they
might rebuild the domestic scene, they might start over on something Egyptian, or they might just jump in the water and play at
being dolphins instead.

It didn't help that they were only in Hawaii at all through
the grace of Phoebe. Her mother had insisted, had simply
bought the entire Paradise Tours package without consulting
with them and handed them the tickets as a wedding gift. In

Phoebe's world, a honeymoon legitimized things. It was simply what one did, it announced to the world that you were serious. But for Rebecca, this mad jaunt just made everything seem surreal. They were lounging around in unsustainable luxury through the munificent whim of a woman with significant neural damage, spending money that wasn't theirs on things they didn't need, having unrealistically idyllic experiences in a place too fantastically beautiful to take completely seriously. Rebecca had moments when she hardly knew whether to feel grateful or dangerously overindulged. She would almost rather have just gone straight back to the foggy house in the Sunset and gotten on with good old chilly real life.

Mike stopped beside her and shook like a happy dog, the drops flying from his ever-longer hair. He'd been bodysurfing for the past hour; he turned out to have a passion for riding the waves in like a kid. The shore break here was abrupt, almost savage, big waves with thousands of miles of ocean behind them welling up for a gorgeous moment before collapsing onto the shallow beach, and Mike's nose and chest were scraped raw from being pounded into the bottom at the end of failed rides. But he was undeterred, and even seemed to like the washing machine tumble at the end of most of his ventures. She loved watching him launch himself with a wave, catching the lift and swell, tapping in to the power of it, and then knifing down along the curling inner edge. Inevitably, she thought of Rory at times: her first husband's best moments had all come offshore.

Mike flopped down beside her. Rebecca could smell the ocean on his skin. His towel was as blue as the Big Island sky and wouldn't last any longer in the real world than hers would. He was wearing a pair of those huge baggy surfer shorts, also like Rory, and he looked completely silly in them, though not any sillier than anybody else did. He tanned easily, Rebecca had learned, to a lovely shade of cinnamon brown. It was amazing to her, in retrospect, that she had married a man without knowing what color he got in the sun. The leaps you took in life, never knowing.

She sat up and licked his shoulder, like a fond cat, tasting salt. "Hey, you."

"Hey, you."

"I feel *completely* decadent."

Mike smiled. "Yeah. It's great."

"No, I mean, really. Seriously. Disso*lute*. It's becoming an issue."

"I'm sure we'll be miserable soon," Mike said, clearly trying to be helpful. He ran a fond finger along the line of her shoulder and, apparently finding her skin inadequately oiled, reached for the suntan lotion. He squeezed a generous puddle of the stuff into his hand and slipped behind her to begin applying it to her back and shoulders. His hands were cool at first, like a breath of the sea, but they warmed quickly on her sun-baked skin.

Rebecca closed her eyes and relaxed into the sensuous glide of his touch. Her cumulative SPF by now was probably in the thousands; Mike rubbed her body at every opportunity. She felt like a beloved car, a ridiculously pampered treasure with thirty-seven coats of paint: waxed, polished, and incessantly buffed. It was wonderful, actually. She'd never felt like an object of such devotion before.

"Isn't there some kind of Bible story about some woman rubbing some expensive oil on Jesus?" she said, trying again.

"Uh-huh," Mike answered absently, his attention at the base of her neck now, the balls of his thumbs sending little reverse shivers upward, like salmon swimming against the stream of her thoughts.

"And the disciples get their panties in a bunch over the waste? Like, they should have sold the oil and given the money to charity or something?"

"This stuff is $1.98 a bottle."

"You know what I mean."

"I suppose," Mike said.

Rebecca knew he would let it go at that. She often tried to lure him into Christian discourse, but he was routinely elusive. She said, "My theological *point,* Brother Jerome, is: Didn't Jesus come down firmly on the side of indulgence?" And, as Mike laughed, "*Seriously.* He backed the woman up, right? Told the disciples to chill out?"

"Well, there's a context," Mike said. He had found a pea-sized knot near the top of her scapula, and his thumb was holding it in tension. Rebecca wondered briefly whether the pressure was a Mike-ishly Zen comment on the parable, a visceral koan fretted on her high-strung musculature; and then she stopped thinking, as the point deepened into a sort of spaciousness under the continued pressure and her whole consciousness went into her body there and opened into somewhere else and then came back.

It felt like it might have been hours. Mike's thumb had moved about a millimeter. The ocean looked like something that had just been invented, a project still in the developmental phase. What a great idea, Rebecca thought: an ocean.

"A 'context'?" she said.

"What Jesus actually said, more or less, was, 'Just think of this as anointing me for burial a little ahead of schedule.' And a couple days later he was dead."

Rebecca laughed. She really hadn't seen that coming, though she probably should have.

She said, affectionately, "I wasn't looking for the stations of the cross, honey, I was just trying to feel better about lying around in the sun like a happy seal."

"You started it," Mike said. "I'm just trying to keep my hands on your body, here."

By the time Phoebe made it to the top of the stairs, she was exhausted. She slumped against the rail on the landing outside the kitchen door to rest. Whoever was destroying the place had settled in to a steady rhythm, and there appeared to be no hurry. Her entire body was bewildered by all this extraordinary effort; her breath came in ragged pants, and her heart was slamming around like a bee in a jar. She could hear another level of sound now in her head that was louder than the crashing, and slightly more vivid, and it made her wonder for a moment whether the crashing was real either. No one told you that you would be able to hear other parts of your brain like that, like noise from a neighboring apartment, sometimes relatively coherent, like an excited conversation, sometimes like a stereo turned up too loud, and sometimes just as a species of pandemonium. Phoebe didn't want to let anyone suspect how chaotic the environment was in her head. It would just upset them. There was such an emphasis, in stroke recovery, on getting back as close as possible to what had once passed for normal; everyone just wanted for you to hurry up and be okay. There was a certain look that came out on Rebecca's face when she realized yet again that Phoebe simply wasn't up to speed anymore, and Phoebe would do pretty much anything she could to avoid provoking it. Unfortunately, there was so much, in the way of incapacity, that you couldn't see coming; and even what capacities she had now were often hit-or-miss. She could sometimes recite entire passages of Shakespeare from memory, as clean and crisp as if a tape recorder were running; and at other times she couldn't sort out Hamlet from an omelet and just wanted to be sure she could get to the bathroom by herself.

A fresh crash from inside the kitchen reassured her that something real was occurring in there. Phoebe reached for the handle and found that the door was locked. She had a key, but keys were one of those things now. She considered her options briefly, decided she would much rather be killed by whoever was trashing the house than try to go back down those stairs, as long as they just let her sit down for a moment first, and lifted her cane to rap firmly on the door.

Shave and a haircut, two bits. The rhythm came automatically and on a wave of resonance. It really was so interesting how your brain worked, once you lightened up about having it work right. Phoebe could remember her father telling her knock-knock jokes when she was five, and how he had laughed uproariously at all the knock-knock jokes she made up then, even though none of them were funny. He'd died of a heart attack, boom, bam, gone. Leave 'em laughing, he'd always said. None of this stroke stuff for him.

Knock-knock. Who's there? Burglar. Burglar who? Burglar with a sledgehammer.

The door opened and Phoebe gripped her cane, prepared to go down fighting, but it was Mary Martha and, behind her, Rory, who was in fact wielding a sledgehammer and had already smashed a ragged hole in the far kitchen wall. No doubt there was a reasonable explanation for that.

"Hello, Gran-Gran," Mary Martha said.

"Hello, sweetheart. Do you have a chair?"

"We moved the chairs into the living room. Daddy's making a hole in the wall."

"I can see that."

"Hi, Pheebs," Rory said cheerfully. "Sorry for the ruckus."

"It's all right," Phoebe allowed. At least she wouldn't have to die now. Or, worse, tell Rebecca that she hadn't been able to dial 911. "Is there a chair available, by any chance?"

"I'll run grab one for you." He hurried out and was back in a moment with one of the exiled kitchen chairs. Phoebe settled onto it gratefully. Mary Martha promptly clambered up onto her lap.

"Mary Martha, go easy on your poor grandmother," Rory said.

"It's all right," Phoebe said, and gave Mary Martha a squeeze with her good arm. Her granddaughter was the only one who didn't treat her like she was made of glass now. Mary Martha's hair smelled of strawberries and cream. These tasty new shampoos. "So, what's going on here?"

"It's a surprise for Mommie," Mary Martha said.

"That's for sure," Phoebe said.

"A sort of wedding gift," Rory explained. "She's been wanting this wall out for years now. This kitchen has always felt like a phone booth."

He was stoned, Phoebe realized. She could tell, since the stroke. Rory had been conspicuously clean for most of the last year, since getting busted for possession the previous autumn. He'd settled in to a steady job as a lifeguard and swimming instructor at a local pool, married his girlfriend well before their new baby was born, and in general was knocking himself out to be a good citizen, a good father, and a good husband—even a good ex-husband, obviously. But he was definitely stoned at the moment. He was very slowed down.

She said, "You didn't tell Rebecca you were going to do this?"

"That would ruin the surprise," Mary Martha said. "You have to promise not to tell too, Gran-Gran."

"I promise," Phoebe said. "Mary Martha, sweetheart, would you run downstairs for me, please, and get my sweater? It's a little drafty up here."

"That's the hole," Rory said. "It's already improving the air circulation."

"Where is it?" Mary Martha asked.

"On the back of my big chair, I think."

Mary Martha hopped off her lap and trotted away on her mission. Once she was out the door, Phoebe looked at Rory and said, "Maybe you should have waited until you were sober to start knocking down the walls."

Rory instinctively considered denying it, then just met her eyes and gave her a slightly rueful smile, not an attitude, just an acknowledgment. Almost no one met her eyes like that anymore, as if she were a fully sentient being.

"It's just a couple hits," he said.

"A couple hits to knock the wall down. How much to finish the job?"

"No, no, it's not like that. It's just been a little more stressful this week, keeping Mary Martha and all."

Phoebe considered her options, which seemed to be limited to making certain hand-wringing noises that he would ignore completely. It wasn't like she could take the sledgehammer out of his hand. What she really wanted to do was tell him how clearly she saw this leading to catastrophe somehow. He was trying too hard to do too much, and he was already starting to fray. To cheat, to cut corners.

She said carefully, "I'm not sure this is such a good idea, Rory."

"Rebecca is going to be thrilled," he said. "Really."

"It's going to be a ... " Phoebe trailed off, groping for the way to say it, knowing that she just sounded like a feebleminded old woman. She had the meaning, it was right there, she could feel it in her brain like grit in an oyster, but her mind couldn't make the pearl for the word fast enough. It was something she'd often felt since the stroke, the agony of impotent lucidity. Cassandra didn't have some special psychic gift. All she had was helplessness. Once you couldn't do anything about it, everything became painfully clear.

"It's going to be fine, Pheebs," Rory said with such warm and genuine affection that she felt like crying.

Mary Martha came trotting back into the kitchen just then with Phoebe's sweater.

"Thank you, sweetie pie," Phoebe said.

"Your shoes are untied, Gran-Gran."

Phoebe looked down. "My goodness, so they are."

"Do you want me to tie them for you?"

"Would you, please?"

Mary Martha knelt and got to work, making her scrupulous loops, the tip of her tongue sticking out, as Rory's did when he concentrated.

"Is that the Bunny or the Rabbit?" Phoebe asked, trying to follow the procedure.

"The Bunny," Mary Martha said. She did something entirely different than Phoebe remembered, and then went through the hole into the burrow, but somehow the knot came out with only one loop.

Rory had come over by now, and he said, "Do you guys know how to do the Teepee?"

"We know the Bunny and the Rabbit," Mary Martha said.

"She knows them better than me," Phoebe said.

"Well the Teepee might be easier for you." Rory took Phoebe's laces. "There's even an easy little rhyme that goes with it. Watch: Make a teepee. Come inside. Pull down tight so we can hide. Around the mountain . . . here we go! Here's my arrow . . . and here's my bow!" He looked up at them. "Bingo! You got it?"

Phoebe and Mary Martha exchanged a glance. Even stoned, Rory had gone way too fast for either of them, and the technique actually seemed much more complicated than any of the Bunny/Rabbit variations; but Mary Martha's look said, fondly, *Indulge him, he's doing the best he can.* Phoebe felt a burst of love for her granddaughter, and a sort of pain at how much she loved her father. It was heartbreaking, how hard they all were trying.

"Got it," she said to Rory.

Rory, satisfied that he had improved the world by one shoelace, turned back to the wall and picked up the sledgehammer. Mary Martha climbed back onto Phoebe's lap. Phoebe had remembered the word she was groping for earlier by now, it was *tragedy,* but that was just how things went, too little, too late. It was just so lovely, for the moment, to hold her granddaughter close, to smell her hair and feel her happiness. And the wall's demolition really was quite a show, once you realized there was no stopping it.

Chapter Four

His mother said unto Jesus, "Son, why have you done this to us?
Your father and I have been sorrowing."
And Jesus said unto her,
"Knew ye not that I must be about my Father's business?"

LUKE 2:48–49

R emembering mine affliction and my misery, the wormwood and the gall...

It was warm enough even at 4:00 AM to sit for prayer on the balcony of their eighth-floor hotel room. This high above the water, the waves were the merest whisper on the rocks, and the stars seemed closer than the hotels across the bay. It was like sitting in the sky. You could smell the ocean, not as the sharp salty tang of northern California, but as a softer balm. You could feel the air around you as a bird might feel it, as an embrace.

It made Mike realize how much of his prayer life he had spent feeling like a mole, a blind thing burrowing relentlessly, often hopelessly, through the recalcitrant densities of self and world: down, and deeper down, and deeper still, into heatless earth, into a blackness ever more alien and profound. And the peace he'd found in prayer, more often than not, had been a miner's austere peace, a surrender, lamp-lit at best, to the incomprehensible call to the cold depths of such darkness. As if to live in God were to become a species of stone.

My soul hath them still in remembrance, and is humbled in me.

Slipping back into the hotel room after his meditation, he would ease the sliding door to the balcony shut and stop to listen to Rebecca breathing. There seemed such a miracle in that: to rise from prayer and step into love. The warm room smelled of gardenias and their lovemaking, of the last wine in the glasses by the bed, of the sandalwood candle that had burned all night and still flickered within its heart of wax. Not stone, but flowers and flame, fruit, and flesh: the true eternity, not of what merely didn't change in time, but of what lived and died in the holy moment. Rebecca's face in that candlelight seemed all the eternity he needed now.

He took the stairs down rather than the elevator, nursing the glow within him, nodding to the night clerk at the front desk, who had been startled to see him at this hour on the first day here, less so the second, and who by now just gave him a smile of graveyard-shift camaraderie and lifted his coffee cup.

Outside, Mike moved along the sidewalk through the deep shadows of ancient banyan trees and across the pedestrian bridge to the island park that protruded into Hilo Bay just across from the hotel. The place was a little miracle, a sort of rocky prayer garden. At the far side of the bridge, two old Japanese men stood twenty feet apart on the seawall with their fishing lines in the water, motionless as twin herons. They nodded impassively, once each, in the etiquette of solitaries, as Mike went by.

Beyond the bridge the island was, deliciously, deserted at this hour. He moved across the dark sand toward the rocks on the far side. The sky over the ocean to the east was just beginning to soften toward gray. Across the bay to the west, the mass of Mauna Kea loomed from the mist above the lights of Hilo, the volcano nothing but a massive mystery in this light, a place where the stars were not.

Mike settled on a flat boulder, smelling the seaweed and the salt, listening to the low wash of the waves and the first cries of waking birds beginning to hunt. Soon the day would make itself real through slow degrees; the mountain behind him would sharpen into form against the purpling sky and then, thrillingly, catch the first rays of the sun, a rose touch at the peak. The red sunlight would flow down the mountain like lava, a relentless wave of descending light, searing the world into color and shape.

It is of the Lord's mercies that we are not consumed, because his com-
passions fail not.

He would even be able to see their hotel room by then, picking it out easily by the twin honeymoon towels, orange and blue, hanging from the railing, and to see the reflection of the lit volcano in the sliding glass door, like a promise, like an echo. And that would be his cue to walk back, against the rising tide of fishermen and dog walkers, joggers and women with strollers and people doing tai chi, hoping, if only for a moment before his buzzing daily mind made the usual crap of it, to be a bit like that sunlight, easing down from the peak of his rosy little mystical moment toward the holy making of the day.

Was it really so impossible that Love could walk the planet? Not at all, it seemed, not in balmy seventy-five-degree weather, not on a honeymoon in Eden. Not I, but Christ in me, could do just fine for a little while, playing at being in the world but not of it, in a two-hundred-dollar-a-night hotel room that someone else was paying for.

Mike smiled at himself. The Word made flesh, eating cheeseburgers in paradise. Still, it was nice to catch a glimpse. Lord, make me an instrument of your peace.

In the afternoons they rented masks and flippers and snorkeled in secret coves, working from a list of secret places they'd found in the tourist magazine in their hotel room. Some of the places were in fact quite isolated and relatively unpopulated; and the hilarity that the word *secret* inevitably took on became one of the thousand small delights of their honeymoon, part of their private lovers' language. They drank secret mai tais, ate secret meals, and lounged on secret beaches; they drove down secret roads to secret destinations. Along with the surreal beauty of the island itself, the ongoing play lent an air of sweet mystery to almost everything. It felt like they were moving around in a country of their own most of the time, a vivid place voluptuous with unsuspected meanings, hidden in plain sight.

Given the general sense of idyll, it was almost a relief to Rebecca to find a problem. It made her feel that she hadn't lost touch with reality completely, that she was not ruined for daily life. The week of pure leisure, like a receding tide, had exposed some rocks at which their life in San Francisco had only hinted, the most prominent being that Mike was a morning person and Rebecca was not. At home this showed mostly in the fact that Mike's early routine was still essentially monastic: he woke without fuss or groaning, and without an alarm, at around four, slipped out of bed to engage in the mysterious inwardness of his meditation, then walked over to the 6:30 mass at the local Catholic church. He would get home again just after seven, smelling faintly of frankincense and fog, to slip back into bed with Rebecca for the remaining fifteen minutes before her own alarm went off. Some days she didn't even know he was gone until he got back. The routine worked perfectly on weekdays and so was more or less invisible; on Saturdays Mike skipped the slightly later morning mass, and they savored the extra time together in bed until Mary Martha came trotting in and the day got started.

Here in Hawaii, in the lovely northwest-facing room with the view of Hilo Bay, their mornings were trickier somehow. Instead of going to mass after his morning meditation, Mike would wander around the shore of the bay in the rising dawn light, and he tended to come back from these jaunts a bit later, well after the sun was up, and far more energized than he did at home. He would bustle happily back into the hotel room bearing two giant cups of Kona coffee from a little stand down by the bay, and a cinnamon-raisin scone for her. A lover's gift, continental breakfast in bed: sweet thoughtfulness. But by their fourth day on the island, Rebecca had begun to see an oblique chastisement in the size of that coffee cup; she felt, ever so mildly and fondly, plied with caffeine and sugar, as if she were supposed to be peppier.

Who knew? Rebecca thought. Mike had a Rory streak in him. It was almost like he was coming back stoned. Apparently the damping effect of Catholicism and the gloom of San Francisco served as a natural check on some wild strain of exuberant nature mysticism in Mike. It didn't help that Hawaii made her feel infinitely more languid. She just wanted to lounge there in the enormous bed, getting the slowest and most gentle start possible on the day, dozing amid the sex-tangled sheets like a walrus on a sunny beach, letting her mind wander through the delicious, obligation-free hours of sunlight ahead.

The irony of having married a contemplative and finding herself aggravated by his excessive energy did not escape her, but the loss of her sense of humor was a key part of the whole problem. Rebecca told herself it was just a girl thing, a function of her heightened expectations, but she found herself increasingly preoccupied, reading signs of tension everywhere and projecting the trend into a future of cumulative catastrophe, the two of them drifting relentlessly toward divorce, cinnamon scone by cinnamon scone. It really shouldn't have been that big a deal. But it hurt to have anything not work on a honeymoon.

. . .

That afternoon, as they drove to another secret beach, Rebecca realized that her brooding had reached critical mass and tipped over into paranoia. Didn't Mike understand that their relationship was doomed? That they had fallen fatally out of sync? But he seemed oblivious, chattering on about an old friend who'd recently gotten back in touch. Mike had gone to seminary with the guy, who had eventually ended up as a parish priest in Los Angeles for a while before having the usual monumental crisis of faith blah blah blah. All of Mike's best friends, it seemed, lived from crisis of faith to crisis of faith. Anyway, the guy had eventually married an ex-nun, and they lived somewhere north of Willits in some exquisite blah blah blah.

"They want us to come up for a visit when we get home," Mike said.

"Uh-huh."

He glanced at her. "Are you okay?"

"Just peachy," Rebecca said.

"You seem a little ... uh—"

"I'm fine. Maybe a bit dozy, I think I might have slept bad somehow last night."

"When we slept," Mike said, arching an eyebrow, referring to their glorious sex life, that irony.

"Yeah."

"Shall we stop somewhere along here and grab a cup of coffee?"

"I don't want any damn coffee," Rebecca snapped, surprising even herself.

Mike looked startled for an instant, then hurt, before he controlled his face and concentrated on the road.

"Sorry," Rebecca said. "It's just … I just don't want any coffee, thanks."

"Sure," Mike said, and drove quietly for a while. She suspected that he was praying. He had told her once he often prayed when he was baffled by their dynamics: just gave it all up to God and waited for grace. At the time Rebecca had been pleased by that. Now it just felt condescending.

The beach was exquisite, a waning crescent of white sand lined with coconut palms, ringing a tiny green cove as intimate as a swimming pool. There was a local family at the far end of the beach's curve, with a bunch of coolers and a big picnic lunch spread, umbrellas, and beach chairs; otherwise they had the place all to themselves. A truly secret spot. A keyhole of heaven. A goddamn postcard.

"Nice," Mike noted, so carefully casual that Rebecca wanted to bite his head off. Which was nuts, of course. She recognized that. She wanted out of this condition; she truly did. She just couldn't see any way out that didn't involve acknowledging the bankruptcy of their relationship, the fatal flaws they'd ignored coming in, too obvious now even for commentary.

Mike took out the sunscreen, holding it like it was a loaded gun and he was afraid it might go off. But he said, still with that same note of perfectly pitched amenability, "Would you like me to—"

"No, thanks, I'm a little sunned out," Rebecca said, striving to match his tone. Maybe they really could just ride through this. Or maybe they were setting patterns of denial now that would haunt their marriage until it fell apart. "I'm just going to go up in the shade and paint for a while, I think."

"Oh," Mike said. "Well. Sure."

Rebecca bent to gather up her sketchbook and watercolors and headed off toward a spot beneath one of the palm trees, where she spread her towel and settled in. Just another blissed-out honeymooner, luxuriating in the natural beauty of the Big Island. Oh, the aquas and the teals. She felt Mike watching her for a moment, in frustration and bafflement, something Rory had never done; but then, like Rory, he turned and took his shirt off, picked up one of their rented snorkeling rigs and a set of flippers, and headed for the water.

She came back to herself as she painted. The green of the trees across the lagoon, which had seemed almost derisive to her, nature's empty ironic loveliness in a relationship world red in tooth and claw, turned first into a technical problem, because this green was *different,* was qualitatively unlike any other she had painted. Considering her initial botches, Rebecca realized that her eye had gotten lazy, that her painted trees, especially the watercolors, had been merely iconic for years now, mysteries shrunk to gestures, like a child's green circles atop a single line of crayon brown for a trunk: just something she got onto the paper as a marker for her brain. This green was so fresh that it made its own demand; it lived, resisting the easy banality, and made her live newly to meet it.

It seemed at first that the problem was dilution, that the watercolors bled too thin. Rebecca tried laying the paint on thick, barely dampened, almost scooped from the palette; but she gradually realized that the green's uniqueness was also contextual, a function of the myriad touches of subtle color that emerged from the original mass of foliage under a slower gaze. Just a bit of orange, not ochre-heavy but apricot-light; a streak of lemony yellow, somehow, not flowers, almost atmospheric; and red, sharp and soft, and more red—fuchsia and ruby, scarlet and pink; and the sky, its unprecedented azure drawing the green toward emerald; and the lagoon's aquamarine, a weightless lucidity softening the gem tone toward verdure; and the italicization of the beach's sun-bleached bone white, sharpening everything.

By the time she had the primary masses of the painting sketched and structured, and her palette swimming with third drafts of the hues, Rebecca realized that she was happy. Not happy, actually, but … something good. Something quiet and strong and even peaceful. The landscape was innocent again, a mystery, escaped from the burden of her projections. Her eye was innocent again, seeing the mystery new; and with her eye, her heart.

It was one of the gifts of these last months with Mike, she knew, the return of her painting life, long relegated to a pile of old canvases in the garage. His presence in her life had somehow led her to find that space again, and that old part of her had reawakened. It sounded so corny, but it was true. He had given her back a crucial part of herself.

She would always be grateful for that, Rebecca thought now, with something almost like nostalgia, even if the marriage failed. She could paint. She could raise Mary Martha, God knew she knew how to be a single mother by now. She had good friends. Maybe she and Mike could even be friends, after the dust settled and they could both acknowledge what a crazy thing it had been that they'd believed they could make a go of it.

Mike was back at the blanket now, drying himself off, or at least moving the water around, with his big blue version of her big red-orange towel. Rebecca had worked herself into such a state of artistic detachment and postdivorce serenity that it was a small shock when he started walking toward her and she realized there were some minor details of the breakup process still to be attended to, like explaining to him how their marriage had failed somewhere between the last cinnamon scone and this idyllic lagoon.

"Hey there," she said as he drew near.

"Hey."

He plopped down beside her with a touch of emphasis, as if asserting his right to do so, as if she might dispute it. She still had her brush in her hand, laden with an early attempt to catch the brown-black of the old lava rocks, and Mike gave her painting an appreciative glance. She thought he was going to say something complimentary, blah blah blah, but instead he leaned back and wrapped his hands around his knees and said, "So, what the hell is going on?"

His tone was so precisely the same pleasant and amiable tone he'd been using all along to slide past their tension that it took Rebecca a moment to register what he'd actually said. She felt a surge of adrenaline, the thrill of *This is it, thank God, at last;* and was horrified to hear herself say, "Nothing."

"'Nothing,'" Mike echoed, meaning, clearly, *Bullshit.*

"I told you, I didn't sleep that well last night." He continued to look at her, not buying it. Rebecca couldn't believe herself what she was saying. It was almost like being possessed: some demon had seized control of her; she was channeling lies.

She looked at her painting, trying to recapture that sense of serene acceptance of the worst truths of her life, that free embrace of reality for better and for worse. It was going to be hard to blame the marriage's demise on Mike's failure to engage her over the issues if she lied to his face when he tried to begin talking about them.

What in the world was she afraid of? They had fought before. Not much, maybe three or four times when the temperature truly climbed into the uncomfortable range, but it wasn't like any of it had been that traumatic, at least not after their first fight, which had blown them apart for weeks. But that had been a blind-shots-in-the-dark getting-to-know-you fight. This was marriage, for God's sake. Mike actually fought fair most of the time; he was patient beyond anything she had ever experienced, right up until he lost his temper and said something so over-the-top that you either had to laugh or walk away for a while. He cooled off fast and could laugh at himself about it all within an hour or two at most. He had a way of limning her shticks that made them seem almost endearing, and a disarming way of copping to most of his own crap without too much fuss and denial. She had never felt safer or realer trying to muddle through things with anyone than she did with him; she had actually considered it one of the unforeseen strengths of their relationship.

There was his disconcerting habit of praying at crucial junctures, of course, of just *stopping,* somehow, at the Gordian knot of the moment, shutting up and letting the dust settle; but even that gave a kind of ritual spaciousness to the fights, once you realized it was happening. It was like counting to ten, or a hundred, or a thousand; it slowed things down and it usually even helped. It was certainly more effective than Rory's old preferred technique of hauling out a giant doobie and lighting up or slamming the door and driving off with a screech of the tires.

Mike was probably praying now, Rebecca realized. His silence had turned stolid, frankly downshifted for the long haul. He was going to wait out the bullshit. And she realized that maybe that, precisely, was it: she didn't want this to be just about her bullshit. She felt incredibly petty; when she boiled it all down and tried to articulate it, it started to sound a lot like they might have avoided all this wretchedness if he had just brought her medium coffees after his morning walk instead of extra large. And that just wasn't it. She wasn't sure quite what it was.

She said, with a touch of rueful self-deprecation, "I think I may be about to get my period too."

Mike held on for another moment without relenting, then he shook his head and stood up.

"What?" she said.

"If you don't want to talk about it right now, we don't have to talk about it now," he said. "But don't treat both of us like fucking idiots."

They drove back to the hotel in silence. It was Mike who was madder now, Rebecca realized, and in a way it took the pressure off. At least she wasn't the only one stewing. It was unnerving, though; her new husband had a previously unsuspected capacity to go completely into some zone of his own, an opaque place with a cold hard shell. She actually felt alone in the car, as if he were a cab driver or something, he was that far away.

Back at the hotel Mike pulled into the numbered space in the parking garage too fast and hit the wall with a sickening crunch of yielding metal, hard enough that Rebecca's head snapped back. She held her breath, thinking that at least now they'd have an exchange of some sort, either to laugh or to explode, but Mike didn't say anything, not even *Shit,* nor did he give her a glance of camaraderie, chagrin, or blame. He didn't back the car away from the impact point either; he just put the parking brake on, turned off the ignition, and got out, as if a whiplash-inducing stop with the bumper crumpled against the concrete was standard parking procedure.

He was already halfway across the parking garage toward the elevator, moving like a man with a mission, by the time Rebecca realized he wasn't going to come around to her side of the car and open the door for her. It had been one of the small delights of their relationship, Mike's unexpected little southernisms, endearing archaic touches of antebellum chivalry, like opening doors and always positioning himself to walk on the traffic side of the sidewalk, as if she might get splashed by a passing carriage.

It took Rebecca several tries to get out of the car herself; the rental had some complex new locking system that required pressing buttons. Mike was out of sight by now. She moved to look at the front of the car and found that the bumper was in fact a total loss. It was one of those clever semiplastic things that disappeared at the merest touch of contact and clearly hadn't been designed for a furious monk in a bad honeymoon moment. She wondered how much she should care, paperworkwise, and decided: not much. It really was a side of Mike she'd never seen before.

•   •   •

When she got back to the room, there was no sign of Mike. Rebecca sat down on the bed and tried to think of what to do next. If she was Mike, of course, she would probably pray, just give it all up to God and rely on His mercy. As things stood, all Rebecca could think to do was either start drinking or call Bonnie Schofield. What an appalling lack of inner resources she had to show for almost four decades on the planet.

She checked the menu, and the room service alcohol cost a fortune, money probably better saved to cover the repairs to the rental car, so she reached for the telephone and dialed her best friend's number. Bonnie wasn't home, and Rebecca couldn't imagine leaving a message that wouldn't sound like someone had died, so she just hung up and tried Bonnie's cell instead. To her relief, her friend answered on the second ring.

"Hey there," Rebecca said.

"Becca! Sweetheart! I was just thinking about you. How *are* you, you little lovebird?"

"Circling the drain, frankly."

"Great!" Bonnie said, so brightly that Rebecca understood that someone else was there. Probably Bob, Bonnie's husband, an earnest, sweet, relatively clueless man; in general, Bonnie swore by his relationship savvy, but in practice she tended to spare him the details.

"Who's there?"

"The whole gang," Bonnie said; and, aside, "In a minute, sweetheart, let me have a turn with her first."

"Mary Martha's there?" Rebecca said. "Where *are* you?"

"Rory's backyard."

"What?!"

"I'm just going to go over here and talk to your mom a minute," Bonnie told Mary Martha on the other end. "No, sweetie, in a minute. You go get another hot dog."

"A hot dog," Rebecca said.

"We're having a barbecue," Bonnie said, dryly now, having apparently established some privacy.

"This is the same Rory we're talking about, right? The one on parole?"

"What can I say? Mary Martha wanted to have a barbecue. She saw it in a movie or something, or on *Mr. Rogers,* I don't know. And I hate to say it, Rebecca, but Rory's looking awfully suburban at the moment. He's got an apron and a chef's hat and everything. He's got a *spatula*. And Mary Martha is eating it up."

Rebecca was silent for a moment. When she had left their daughter for this week with her ex-husband and his relatively new wife Chelsea, she had had any number of concerns, but they had mostly centered around drug abuse and criminal neglect, the possibility of Social Services stepping in and prosecuting them all for blatant failures of parenthood. She certainly hadn't foreseen worrying about losing Mary Martha's domestic affections to some kind of stoner's version of Ozzie and Harriet.

"But seriously—" she said.

"If it makes you feel any better, he's overcooking everything."

Rebecca decided to worry about it later. "Bonnie, we're having a big fat stupid fight."

"That bastard," Bonnie said, instantly supportive.

"No, no, I think it's mostly my fault."

"Hmm—" Bonnie began contemplatively, but then, aside again, "No, no, take a number, honey."

"Who—?"

"Yo' mama," Bonnie said. "Damn, she's insisting."

"Phoebe's there? Shit, Bonnie, *no*—"

"Hello, sweetheart," her mother said.

Rebecca could picture the transaction. Phoebe had no doubt simply taken the phone out of Bonnie's hand. She said, resignedly, "Hi, Mom."

"Is everything all right?"

"Of course everything's all right. We're having a blast. We bless you every day and light candles of gratitude for this perfect gift."

"No need to get sarcastic. Bonnie had a look on her face."

"That's just Bonnie's normal look. She had a tricky childhood."

Phoebe hesitated briefly, possibly trying to decide whether that had been a shot. Rebecca hastened to say, "Everything's great, Mom. Really."

"Silly me," Phoebe said. "To suspect that someone with your naturally serene and sunny disposition could possibly have a moment's trouble in the stressful early days of a new marriage."

Rebecca considered bursting into tears and telling her everything. Phoebe could handle it, even poststroke. But she could picture the scene in Rory's backyard, which was about seventeen square feet of dead grass, normally inhabited by Bruno, Rory's enormous and overly affectionate chocolate Lab, and dangerously rife with Bruno's defecations. There was no way Phoebe could be in anything approaching a truly private space, and this was no time to set off alarms among the general populace.

"It's all good, Mom," she said, ruefully enough that she knew Phoebe would take it both as an acknowledgment and as reassurance that Rebecca felt she could work it out. "How are *you?*"

"Well, I'm fine, I suppose. Bonnie has been wonderful. Too wonderful, even. She calls every day and stops by after work. And Rory and Mary Martha have been by quite a bit too."

"Rory and Mary Martha have been by the house?"

There was a silence, slightly unnerving. Rebecca could never tell anymore whether Phoebe's pauses were diplomatic, tactical, or stroke related. In the past, a silence like this would have spoken volumes, and Rebecca couldn't help but suspect that it still did.

She said, "You can't talk about it right now, can you?"

"Nope," Phoebe said.

"Should I get on the next plane?"

"No, dear, you just enjoy yourself. It can wait until you get home."

"I'm serious."

"Me too.... Mary Martha's standing here jumping up and down like a Mexican bean."

"I guess you'd better put her on, then. These are Bonnie's minutes we're using up here."

"Your father threw a clock against the wall on our honeymoon, you know," Phoebe said.

"Really? You never told me that."

"I'm sure it was just symbolic," Phoebe said. "Tempus fugit or something. Of course it freaked *me* out. But what did I know? I was only nineteen."

Rebecca laughed. "I love you, Mom."

"I love you too, sweetheart. Here's our angel."

"Mommy?" came Mary Martha's eager voice.

Rebecca gathered herself to be a decent mother herself. "Hi there, honeybaby. How are *you?*"

"We're having a barbecue!"

"How *wonderful.* Is it sunny there?"

"No, it's foggy. But it's warm if you stand by the fire."

"And you're eating hot dogs?"

"And a bite of hamburger. Bruno ate the rest of it but I didn't mind. And chips. And Pepsi."

"Potato salad?" Rebecca asked, just to yank her chain.

"Mo-om!"

"Just kidding."

"I *hate* potato salad."

"I know, honey. What's for dessert?"

"Gran-Gran brought cookies, and Chelsea made a chocolate cake."

Rebecca rode past the pang. It was hard to picture Chelsea, a sweet twenty-something posthippie Deadhead, cooking anything more complicated than a microwave burrito. But apparently you couldn't turn your back for a second. "A *chocolate* cake. Wow. Perfect. Your favorite."

"I've got to go," Mary Martha said matter-of-factly, a child's mind attending to the moment in front of her. "I'm Daddy's assistant."

"Okay, honey. Have fun. I love you love you love you."

"I love love you you," her daughter said, and the phone clicked off.

So much for the support and perspective of friends and family. Rebecca didn't know whether to be relieved or not that Mary Martha hadn't given the phone back to Bonnie. But at least her daughter hadn't handed it to Rory.

Rebecca set the receiver down and reached for the room service menu again. The liquor hadn't gotten any cheaper. But she'd already used up plan B. She decided to save the service fee, delivery charges, and double tip, and headed downstairs to the bar.

T he Aloha Wai'Ona was all bamboo and floppy fronds, with waitresses in grass skirts and a view of the bay out the broad open doors onto the patio. Rebecca sat down at the tiki hut bar with her back to the sunset and said in a let's-get-down-to-business tone to the bartender, "What's good?"

The guy, a fresh-faced young local in a spectacular pink and purple aloha shirt that somehow looked natural on him, considered briefly, then said, "Speaking as a tourist, a connoisseur of fine liquors, or a woman looking for adventure?"

Rebecca laughed. "Speaking as a newlywed on her honeymoon in Paradise, in the middle of the first idiotic fight of her marriage."

"Ah, that's easy, then."

"Is it?"

"Apple martini." He got to work immediately and made a bit of a theatrical production out of it, right down to cutting a fresh slice of apple and dumping the ice from the chilled glass with a flourish the instant before he poured the drink. The glass was hand painted to look like a little palm tree. Rebecca picked it up by the curved trunk and sipped.

"Wow," she said. "The green apple makes it."

"Not just green apple," the guy said. "Granny Smith."

She raised her glass. "You are a prince among men."

"*Kâmau,*" the guy said.

"'*Kâmau*'?"

"Ancient Hawaiian toast," he said. "In context, roughly, You go, girl."

Rebecca laughed appreciatively, and he gave her a grin and moved off to get back to making mai tais for the accumulating cocktail hour crowd. The sunset was in progress and the outside patio was filling up fast.

Rebecca sipped her drink tentatively, not quite sure how drunk she wanted to get with Mike AWOL. Her impulse was to damn the torpedoes and charge without delay toward a maudlin stupor, but she suspected that was just the power of cliché talking. What she really wanted was for everything to be all right again between her and Mike as soon as possible, before things got any crazier.

From her stool she could just see the volcano across the bay, with the sun easing toward it and the first pinks starting to come out on the clouds. The light glittered on the water and birds swirled in the fragrant air. Almost everyone at the bar was outside enjoying the scene. There was one younger couple at a table by the near wall who looked like they had only gotten out of bed long enough to eat and might not stay through the end of the salad course, and a lovely older couple in their sixties, sitting contentedly at a table with a view out the door, holding hands.

It took her some time to notice that there was one other guy inside the bar, at a dim table in the farthest corner. Rebecca actually had to look twice to realize it was Mike. He was sitting beneath an unlit tiki torch contemplating a bottle of Budweiser, oblivious to everything else. He looked almost comically like Humphrey Bogart with his gin in *Casablanca:* All the honeymoon hotels on all the tropical islands in all the world, and she walks into mine.

Rebecca got the bartender's attention on his next pass and said, "I want to send a drink to that guy in the corner."

"Is that the Husband, or are you cutting your losses and branching out?"

"I'm going to give him one more chance."

"Done," the guy said, and reached for the martini shaker.

"No, no, just a beer," Rebecca said. "He drinks Bud."

The bartender just gave her a look, like, Give me a break, and continued making the apple martini. Rebecca surrendered herself to the apparently inevitable and settled back to watch what went into the drink, trying to memorize the recipe in case this turned out to be some kind of magic formula. Lemon squeeze, lime squeeze, a generous dose of Stoly, some sour apple schnapps, and a touch of Midori melon liqueur. Her parents, martini purists, would have been horrified. The bartender poured the drink off into the chilled glass with his usual flourish, sliced a perfect slab of Granny Smith apple and floated it niftily, then flagged a waitress, nodding toward Mike. Rebecca waited a beat to give her a head start, then rose to follow. She figured she'd arrive on the heels of the drink, for maximum effect.

"I'm here for you if it doesn't work out," the bartender said.

Rebecca paused to give him an amused glance. He was, she reckoned, about six percent serious, maybe eight.

"I'm flattered, you sweet young thing," she said. "Your tip will be enormous."

He smiled. "In that case, the drinks are free."

She started across the room, feeling heartened by that exchange. It seemed like a sign that maybe things had really bottomed out.

As she approached the table, the waitress was taking the opportunity to relight the tiki torch above Mike's head. The woman seemed a little put out and rolled her eyes slightly at Rebecca as she came up, a girl thing, as if to say, Okay, now he's *your* problem. Rebecca realized that Mike had probably extinguished the thing somehow, in the service of his gloom. For some reason, that made her love him more.

Mike waited until the waitress had moved off, then met Rebecca's eyes and said, a trifle ruefully, "Hello, Mrs. Christopher."

His eyes in the lamplight were rich, warm brown, deeper and sweeter than the darkest chocolate. How you could forget something as fundamental and crucial as the flavor and feeling of your lover's eyes? Saying "brown" to yourself in his absence, as if that meant something. When all that really meant anything was being with him.

"Hello, Mr. Christopher," Rebecca said, and sat down beside him.

Mike took her hand at once, delicately, holding just the first two fingers, his thumb testing the knuckle of her index finger as if it were important to assess any interim changes; and then he raised her hand to his lips and kissed it.

"How's the car?" he said.

Rebecca smiled. "I think it will still run."

"How's the *wall?*"

She laughed. "The wall won, honey. The wall's fine." And, as he continued to look chagrined, "If it's any consolation, it looked to me like you weren't the first one to have hit it."

"I'm *so* sorry."

"It's okay."

"No, not about the car. About us. About me."

"I know," she said. "I'm sorry too."

They were silent a moment. He was still holding her hand by the fingers, and Rebecca looped her thumb up to cover his. It seemed to her that she was breathing again, that she hadn't breathed in about six hours.

Mike was looking at the drink, as if noticing it for the first time. "What *is* this?"

"Apple martini."

He laughed. "An *apple* martini?"

"It wasn't me, I swear, it was the bartender. I ordered you a beer."

"That's what Eve said, I think."

"Nobody's making you drink it. Which is *also* what Eve said."

He gave her a smile and pointedly took the apple slice out of the drink to take a bite. "Whoa," he said. "That's not gin."

"That's what Adam said."

"Well, then, we'd better start looking for some fig leaves, I guess." He raised his glass. "To … the loss of innocence?"

"Kâmau," Rebecca seconded.

"'*Kâmau*'?"

"I got it from the bartender. It means something like, You go."

"I thought the bartender was Satan."

"You say that like it's a bad thing," she said. "If this doesn't work out, actually, I think I've got a shot with him."

•   •   •

The next day, their last on the island, they went to see the volcano. They'd been told that Kilauea was in a phase of eruption, actual lava flow, and that it was a unique opportunity and so forth, but they almost stayed in bed all day anyway. They had a room service breakfast delivered midmorning and were actually considering a room service lunch by the time they finally decided to rouse themselves for a final act of tourism.

They had been told that the walk to see the place where the lava flow met the sea was quite long, and so they didn't linger in the visitor's center over the postcards and trinkets and educational displays on the science of the earth's tectonic plates; nor did they pause long at the edge of the awesome Kilauea crater. The drive down to the sea wound through stretches of recent lava flows, entire districts buried beneath fresh black rock, like the scorched landscape of a planet too close to the sun. They had wondered how they would know when it was time to walk, but it was quite clear when they arrived at their takeoff point: a recent flow had crossed the road, and the highway stopped without ceremony at the edge of a plain of new stone.

They parked beside the road with the dozens of other rental cars that the promise of spectacle had drawn. A big sign warned them of the danger of toxic gas, heat vents, and collapsing shelves, absolved the relevant entities of any and all responsibility in the event that they should die a terrible flaming death, and advised them to wear sturdy shoes.

They set out across the pathless rock, walking tentatively at first: the ground felt so freshly made that it was likely still hot. Within moments they were out of sight of the road and there was nothing but the pillowy crumplings of the recently hardened lava and the ocean to their right, the usually idyllic flavor of its blue-green made primeval somehow by the rawness of the new coast. Rebecca found her mind trying to wrap itself around the extraordinary nature of the place and finally surrendering. It was like nothing else, a place without history, without births and deaths, without soil, even. There was nothing for the mind here but fear and awe. It could have been any moment in the last four billion years, or the next four billion. This was just how the earth looked, newly born.

They used up their exclamations quickly, and after that they walked in silence, holding hands when they could, releasing each other briefly to scramble up little rises and down sharp slopes. It was quiet and hot, a baking heat completely different from the usual mild wet Hawaiian warmth.

After about half a mile they spotted a cluster of people up ahead. They slowed as they approached; there was something odd about the group, something Rebecca couldn't quite place at first. And then she realized that no one was talking. Almost two dozen tourists armed with cameras and the usual platitudes, and none of them saying a word. They were rapt, reverent, and silent.

Mike and Rebecca made their way to an open spot along the edge of the little cliff where everyone had stopped. Below them was an amazingly normal looking beach of pale sand, overhung with the miniature massif of the accumulated stone. A single lumpen boulder at the waterline seemed the furthest advance of the lava; as Rebecca watched, a wave broke, ran up to the boulder, and exploded into steam. A moment later, from the overhang above the rock, a languid dollop of sluggish stone—red, she realized, glowing live red—oozed into prominence, stretched itself into a drop, and fell, splattering on the boulder in a fresh spray of steam.

A murmur ran through the gathered tourists. New earth, Rebecca thought, as new as it could be, right there. The planet making itself. What seemed most amazing to her at that moment was how *slow* it was, the measured, relatively minuscule bit of that liquid stone that had made its molten way from somewhere toward the center of the planet, emerging for its instant of exposure and assuming its surface nature as the substance of the earth. She looked at Mike and he met her eyes and she thought, We will always remember this.

They stayed for almost half an hour without saying a word. Other people came and went; some even arrived chattering, in several different languages, but the group never lost its quiet air of spontaneous awe. By the time they left, the stone on the beach had almost doubled in size.

As Mike and Rebecca made their way back toward the car, she could feel the prayer in his silence, and for once she felt in sync with it, beyond the superfluities and the nonsense, able to relate. She took his hand, and he gave her a smile, raised her fingers to his lips, and kissed them, and she felt that as a kind of prayer as well.

Chapter Five

Bear ye one another's burdens, and so fulfill the law of Christ.

LUKE 2:48–49

I
t was one of the days when things were not entirely clear. Rory had driven them to the airport, but Phoebe wasn't sure why. She didn't want to ask, because she was afraid it would reveal the degree of her confusion, which would only upset everyone. She decided to just wait it out and see what developed. Some of the planes carried the living, and some carried the dead: arrivals and departures. She thought perhaps it was her time to go, and thank God for that if it was so. But maybe it was Rory's. He had death written all over him now, but she could not say that. God did not work that way. Her words weighed nothing anymore. She had died already, and her speech was the speech of the dead. She had done her three days in the grave, and the Lord had called her back for reasons she could not really understand at all.

They didn't teach that at church. No one had mentioned this phase at all. She had been trying to find out more about Lazarus, who had been in the grave so long he stank when Jesus called him back. But nobody knew anything about Lazarus. It was the miracle that mattered to them, the miracle, apparently, that was the point. Or maybe Jesus had just done it to make the sisters happy. Phoebe wondered how long Lazarus had had to hang around after that, and whether he had ever said anything to anyone about all the other stuff, and if anyone had written it down. It didn't seem like it. And what good would it do anyway? Dead was dead, even if you were still walking around. No one alive could hear her unless she spoke the language of the alive. But all the truth she knew now seemed to come out in the language of the dead.

They were walking, and it was endless. There were people everywhere, it was a circle of hell, and the damned stood in lines that were endless to go nowhere. But Rory seemed to know where they were going. Phoebe just held Mary Martha's hand. Mary Martha was one of the clear places. With Mary Martha it was possible to remember and her head was quiet. Rory's girlfriend was with them, and the new baby, but those were not clear places or places of quiet. Rory was not stoned, and so he was not a clear place either. That was part of the sadness. This was not hell, it was an airport. That was part of the sadness too. Because airports were worse. At least in hell you burned in God. This burning just went round and round like a wheel. It was a burning in a hurry.

Now they were somewhere, because they had stopped. It's me or you, Rory, Phoebe thought, and I just hope it's me. But it was an arrival, Rebecca, with flowers around her neck, and Mike with her. Rebecca, lit with happiness. And Mike, who was the clearest place. He met Phoebe's eye, the way no one did anymore, and winked. He spoke the language of the dead like her, she knew. And he too had learned to keep his big mouth shut.

You just never know, Phoebe thought, hugging her daughter, using the English airport words that came so easily from somewhere that seemed to always know exactly what to say to the living. *I really should stop trying to figure it out.* But this brain of hers, it just went on and on, like a coffee grinder. The body too, surprise, surprise. And what a pain that was.

I guess the honeymoon is over, Rebecca thought. Not that she hadn't known that it would be—eventually, inevitably, and probably quickly. But she really hadn't expected the end to be quite so immediate and emphatic.

The banner stretched across the rupture in the kitchen wall read "Welcome Home Mommy and Mike," with each letter a different color, and clearly Mary Martha had put almost as much work into it as Rory had into destroying the wall. Beyond the ragged gap, Phoebe, Bonnie and Bob Schofield, and a dozen other friends stood in the weird new immediacy of the dining room amid the debris, tools, and construction materials, with champagne glasses raised and big Queen-for-a-Day This-Is-Your-Life-Rebecca grins on their faces, except for Phoebe, who looked uneasy enough to suggest that she understood what was actually going on.

"Surprise!" Mary Martha sang out. It really had been brilliant on Rory's part to get her so deeply involved, and to have so many witnesses present. It was going to be awkward, at best, to kill him now.

"My, my, my," Rebecca said, to buy some time.

"Obviously there's still some work left to be done," Rory said modestly. "But you get the basic idea already."

"I sure do." Rebecca accepted a flute of champagne from Bonnie. "I'm speechless," she said to the assembled guests, who cheered and, mercifully, started drinking and chattering. Rebecca stood just inside the kitchen accepting greetings and welcomes and congratulations, unable to move yet from the spot where she had first glimpsed the new decor. Fortunately, everyone seemed so happy with the situation that there didn't seem to be much required on her part except to not begin screaming at her ex-husband. She concentrated on that.

After the first wave of attention had passed, Mike took the opportunity to sidle up to her and murmur, in a tone that indicated he was trying hard to be supportive but had his doubts, "Did I miss something?"

"No more than me," Rebecca said.

"You asked him to do this?"

"Eight *years* ago." It had been during Rory's last attempt at being a good citizen. They had just moved into the house, and Rebecca was pregnant with Mary Martha. Briefly sobered by their impending parenthood, Rory had gotten an actual job, doing something with insulation, and for a month and a half he had thrown himself into a normality so determined, spectacular, and self-conscious that it had a note of parody. The kitchen expansion project then had symbolized the new, responsible, constructive Rory, but by the time Mary Martha had been born, he'd already lost the insulation job and was spending ten hours a day in the ocean, ostensibly training for the West Coast surfing championships, and the kitchen wall remained undisturbed.

"I'm going to go have a cigarette," Mike said. "Or two. Or three. Let me know when the party's over."

"Coward."

"Yup," he said, and slipped out the back door. A flawless escape; it barely made a ripple in the party. Rebecca had long since noted how good Mike was at that sort of social disappearance. Obviously one reason he had lasted so long in the monastery was that he really didn't like crowds.

"Is he okay?" Bonnie asked, coming up with a fresh glass of champagne for Rebecca. Being Bonnie, she was the only one who had noticed the getaway.

Rebecca shrugged. "He's Mike. He just wants things to quiet down so that he can do his vespers meditation and get in bed."

"This is really sort of for the two of you." Bonnie's tone had a trace of disapproval. For all her general tolerance and support, she had distinct ideas about proper marital behavior.

"I think he feels like he paid his dues already by showing up at the church instead of staying out there in the woods in his hut."

As if on cue, to illustrate a good husband doing his social duty, Bob joined them just then, also with a fresh glass of champagne for Rebecca. "Oops," he said, seeing that she already had one.

"It's okay," Rebecca said, accepting the extra drink. She thought she could either take it out to Mike at some point or put it to good use herself. She'd drunk one glass so far, and by that fizzy light the muddling of the kitchen already seemed more like gratuitous damage than wanton destruction. She wondered if Rory had removed any weight-bearing pillars. She wondered if he even knew what a weight-bearing pillar was. Structural integrity had never been his strong suit.

"So how was Hawaii?" Bob asked.

"Wonderful," Rebecca replied, feeling the magic fading already, like the life from one of those colorful reef fish, caught and mounted on a board.

"I'll bet it was. We'll have to have you guys over for dinner soon, and properly debrief you."

"That would be great," Rebecca said, with what she hoped was an appropriate degree of polite vagueness.

"When are you free? How about next Friday?"

Rebecca glanced at Bonnie and found no help there. Bonnie thought Bob was great. It was very moving, in its way, after so many years of dating losers, of Bonnie saying that all she wanted was a decent man who cared about her and she would be content. It had turned out to be true. Bob was decent in the extreme, and Bonnie was content. Rebecca was happy for her friend, but unfortunately she thought Bob was an ass. It had hamstrung what had once been a deep and freewheeling friendship. It didn't help that

Rebecca had had first shot at Bob and had passed without a second thought. Fortunately, that never came up. Bonnie had caught Bob on the short hop of his rebound and never looked back.

"I'll make my famous garlic asparagus and pasta with lemon cream," Bob persisted.

"Well—"

"Bob's started making his own pasta," Bonnie chimed in. "It's amazing."

"I think it just adds incredible character to the meal," Bob said modestly.

"I've felt stymied for years by a lack of character in my noodles," Rebecca said, and when neither of them even smiled, she cut her losses and said, "I'll have to check with Mike, of course."

"And we know how crammed *his* schedule is," Bonnie agreed, and she and Bob giggled in a way that made Rebecca realize that the poverty of Mike's social life—and work life too, perhaps—had been a topic of some discussion.

"We'll pencil you in, at least," Bob said. "Seven, say?"

"Light pencil. Very light."

"Of course. Any preferences on the wine?"

"High alcohol content."

"That white Bordeaux was perfect last time," Bonnie said.

"Or a Loire sauvignon blanc," Bob agreed. "Depending on whether I go with the rotini or try a spinach mafalda."

"Surprise me," Rebecca said.

•   •   •

Phoebe had been rather conspicuously keeping her distance, but Rebecca finally caught up with her in the dining room, where her mother was sitting on one of the exiled kitchen chairs beside Rebecca's drawing table. Everything in the room, which Rebecca had been using as the workshop for her graphics business, was covered with big sheets of plastic, which in turn were covered by a thick layer of drywall dust. It looked like something from the aftermath of Pompeii.

"Welcome home, sweetheart," her mother said.

"You knew about this?"

Phoebe shrugged. "Mary Martha made me promise not to tell."

"He's using that kid like a crowbar."

Her mother didn't disagree. "He said he'd be done by the time you got back."

"And you believed him?"

"Of course not."

It was heartening, somehow, to know that Phoebe had not lost her mind entirely. And Rebecca could more or less picture the scene. No doubt there had been no stopping Rory once he had the sledgehammer out.

"What on *earth* got into him?" she said.

"I think he really did want to do something nice for you. And I think there's a touch of ... damn, what's the word—?"

"Vandalism?" Rebecca prompted. Her mother's meanderings through the vague depths of her rearranged brain still unnerved her. Since the stroke, she had realized how much she had always relied on Phoebe's brisk articulateness. To see it falter shook her world much more than she could have anticipated. "Revenge? Insanity?"

"No, no, it's on the tip of my tongue.... *Damn.*" Phoebe was silent again, then said, "I really should have died on the sidewalk that day."

"And missed my wedding?" Rebecca said, trying to keep it light. "How rude."

"You weren't even engaged at that point," Phoebe said. "I should have gotten hit by a truck."

"Don't talk like that, Mom. You've got a lot of life left in you."

"It's best to leave 'em laughing," Phoebe said. "Like my father. Like *your* father. Even Jesus."

"Jesus left them laughing?" Rebecca said dubiously.

"It's a very dry humor, sweetheart."

Rebecca laughed in spite of herself. If Phoebe could still talk like that, she felt, she had a good run left in her.

Rory approached them just then. He still had Mary Martha by his side, like a very short bodyguard, both of them still aglow with their good deeds. There was nothing to do for the moment but be a decent mother.

"Mary Martha, that banner is *beautiful,*" Rebecca said. "I still can't get over how you made the letters look like a rainbow."

"Daddy made the letters and I colored them in."

"Well, you guys did a great job."

"I helped him with the wall, too."

"Every kid's dream," Rory smiled. "A hammer, and something to wreck."

Rebecca said, "Mary Martha, sweetie, would you run up to Mommy's bedroom and get the presents I brought back for everyone? They're in that bag beside the blue suitcase."

"Presents!" Mary Martha trotted off through the hole in the wall toward the stairs. The flow-through kitchen really did change the routing through the house.

As soon as she was out of earshot, Rebecca turned to Rory. "So where's the stove?"

"In the living room."

"And the refrigerator?"

"Don't worry, I ran an extension cord to it, it's still running." And, at her look, "There was stuff flying all over the place, Rebecca. I really had to get them out of there."

"Any chance of getting them back soon?"

"Well, there's no sense moving the stove back until we get the gas thing worked out."

"The gas thing."

"I capped off the pipe as soon as I realized it was there, no biggie. There was never any danger."

"*Redemption,*" said Phoebe abruptly, with evident satisfaction. She had been sitting there quietly lost inside herself the whole time they were talking. Rebecca and Rory gave her startled glances.

"Amen, sister," Rory said fondly, lacking a context.

Rebecca met her mother's eyes. It was so strange, these days. Sometimes Phoebe was there, sometimes she wasn't. But she was all there now. So much so that Rebecca half-suspected her mother had had the word the whole time and had been saving her best shot with it until the conversation with Rory threatened to spin out of control.

She said, "Mother, you are a devious, devious woman."

"You have no idea," Phoebe said.

Rory, not sure what was going on but recognizing an opportunity to change the tone, said, "Becca, Chelsea wants to have you guys over for dinner soon."

"Oh?" Rebecca said, trying hard to picture it.

"She's been learning to cook. She wants to try out Phoebe's lasagna recipe."

Phoebe's lasagna recipe, Rebecca knew, was delicious and un-screw-up-able. She knew because it had been the first thing she learned to cook too, and the mainstay of their dinner menus during the early years of her relationship with Rory.

"Well, sure, of course," she said.

Rory whipped a pocket calendar out of his back pocket. "How about next Friday?"

Rebecca blinked. Rory with a pocket calendar. She had a sense of the world having gotten too weird for her, too quickly. "Uh, I think we're already booked up with Bonnie and Bob that night."

"How about the next Friday? Or Saturday, maybe?"

"The Saturday's probably better. I'll have to talk to Mike, and check his schedule."

"I'll pencil you in for Saturday, the ninth."

"That's a pen."

"It's metaphorical, Bec."

She met his eyes, amused in spite of herself. Rory had Mary Martha's sweet blue eyes. Or rather, of course, Mary Martha had his. That, his undeniable intelligence, and his indestructible sense of humor had always made it impossible to completely hate him.

"Did you notice that it's going to be arched?" Rory said.

Rebecca looked at the hole in the wall. She hadn't noticed before—her sense of the damage had been more or less undifferentiated—but in fact there was the first crude approach to an arch across the top of the breach. Eight years ago that had been her stylistic vision; for some reason an arched passage had seemed so elegant to her then.

She had a sudden sense of the bittersweetness of her shared history with Rory, all those visions and hopes shared and broken, all the suffering experienced together, and the suffering caused. There really was no such thing as a fresh start; a second marriage was built on the ruins of the first, as the first was built on the ruins of previous boyfriends. The archeology of love only got more layered and mysterious with every new construction. And, apparently, her relationship with Rory was still a work in progress.

"I know I haven't really thanked you properly yet," she said.

"It's okay. I understand you have to get past the initial shock. But I swear, Becca, I'll get it finished up this weekend, and it's going to be gorgeous."

"It's already gorgeous, it's a beautiful, thoughtful gift," Rebecca said. "But it would be nice if you could get the stove working again soon."

P hoebe was trying to figure out a way to get out the back door without going through the construction materials, which would snag her walker. But every time she pictured walking out of the dining room in the other direction and going down the hall and around, she ended up in the old house in New Jersey where she had lived with her husband for almost forty years. She had two martinis, very dry; it was the end of the day, the cocktail hour, and she could smell the sweet, slightly fruity smoke of John's pipe. They always did their best talking during the cocktail hour, chewing over the day together, digesting it into something that made sense—or even didn't make sense, if it came to that. As long as they had chewed it over together and could smile about it and loved each other still.

"You okay, Pheebs?"

It was Rory, in very clear focus, which meant he had slipped off somewhere and had a hit or two. Phoebe said, "It depends on what year it is."

Rory laughed appreciatively, thank God. Definitely stoned. Phoebe understood. Such lucidity, however temporary, was price-less. But priceless things cost everything in the long run. She said, "If it's not 1971, I would appreciate it if you would help me to the back door."

"Of course," Rory said. He held out his hand for hers and helped her up, then eased her without fuss through the whirls and eddies of the party, across the hazards of the piles of tools, debris, and lumber. She'd known Rory for over fifteen years now and she'd always liked him, even after it became clear that it was time for Rebecca to move on. He had a gentle spirit and a giant heart. And he'd been good for Rebecca, for about fifteen minutes in the mid-eighties.

Her husband, of course, had always wanted to kill him. But you couldn't kill the father of your grandchild, however much you might like to.

At the back door Rory held the door for her. "Are you done for the night or just taking a break?"

"My whole life is a break now," Phoebe said.

Rory laughed again. She hadn't particularly meant to be funny, but it was better than most of the alternatives, and she took advan-tage of the light moment to ease out onto the back porch by her-self. Rory, bless his heart, let her go without a fight, and as soon as the door closed behind her the sky was the sky was the sky was the stars forever and amen. Her face felt like a cramped muscle, knotted into the proper benevolent at-a-party expression. Phoebe was not even sure what the right expression was most of the time anymore, but her face always knew. Her mother had been a stickler for the social graces, and the old disciplines still served; seventy-some years of training in maintaining appearances had not been wasted. And then one day you suddenly found yourself wandering around behind the appearances, like an actor backstage, grateful for the privacy while the play went on up front.

A cigarette flared at the top of the steps and she knew it was John, who had smoked like a fiend and had it kill him early, just like they said it would. But John was dead and gone and she was dead and here like the last rumble of thunder from long-past lightning and it was Mike.

"Hey, handsome," Phoebe said.

"Hey, gorgeous."

She crossed the porch and went through the procedure of getting herself seated on the top step beside him. Mike just let her do it by herself, for which she was grateful. It was use it or lose it; nobody seemed to get that, in their haste to help. You started letting them do it for you, and the next thing you knew you couldn't do it at all.

When she was finally settled, she took a good long while to get her breath back and the stars and the stars and the stars and the sky and Mike didn't say a word. She could smell the jasmine by the fence. It was too cold for jasmine in New Jersey. The winters took it, every time. But that just made the smell of lilacs sweeter in the spring.

"Lemme outta here," Phoebe said.

"Me too."

"No, I mean *really*. Out like a candle. Gone gone gone."

"I'd settle for a good bar," Mike said, and then they were silent again and the stars and the stars and the sky.

Having managed to not kill her ex-husband, Rebecca felt free to just circulate among her friends and have a good time. She was vague about several more dinner invitations; everybody wanted to have her and Mike over, the two of them were the flavor of the month suddenly, and she foresaw, uneasily, a series of initiation ordeals. She had no idea how Mike would handle it all. In all her imaginings, hopes, and worries in marrying an ambivalently resocialized ex-monk, she had not anticipated that particular twist of coupledom. She'd been too worried over whether he was going to renounce the corrupted flesh entirely and go back to the monastery, wear hair shirts, or be weird about God in some other, fatal, way. His ability to make and endure small talk had simply not come up.

As things started to wind down, Bonnie, Bob, and Rory began gathering up glasses and plates and doing the dishes. The unprecedented sight of Rory helping to clean up went a long way toward reconciling Rebecca with the news that his heroic labors had screwed up the kitchen pipes somehow and they were having to do the party dishes in the small downstairs bathroom sink.

Mary Martha and her mother had disappeared, but Rebecca found them both out on the back porch when she went out to tell Mike that the coast was clearing. Mary Martha was sitting on his lap, playing with his hair and chattering animatedly about something that involved red and green animals. Phoebe was sitting beside him on the top step, sipping a glass of champagne that she really shouldn't have been drinking and looking relaxed and contented in a way that she did only around Mike, since the stroke.

The three of them were so beautiful together that Rebecca paused in the doorway to savor the sight. Mike had been great with Mary Martha from the start; the only reason she had rented him the in-law apartment at all, when he had showed up the year before fresh out of the monastery with an escaped-convict's stubble on his recently shaved head and an air of impenetrable gloom, was that Mary Martha had taken to him instantly, and he to her. Rebecca had intended to rent the apartment to a temperate, solidly employed person of demonstrable stability, preferably a woman, and Mike had been homeless, jobless, and literally penniless, with nothing but a small black satchel that contained everything he owned and a comically inadequate severance check of some sort from the monastery, which he couldn't get cashed because all of his forms of ID had been expired for fifteen years. Rebecca had actually heard his stomach growling at the initial interview for the apartment: he'd been sleeping in the park for three days by then and hadn't eaten since God knew when. She had fed him a bowl of Cheerios, Mary Martha had showed up and had one of her own, and the two of them had bonded around some kind of unicorn offer on the back of the box. And that had been that. He'd been late on the second month's rent, but he'd gotten a job at McDonald's by then and was regular thereafter, and there had never been any doubt that he was the quietest tenant she would ever find. It was, of course, the quiet ones you had to watch out for.

Mary Martha said something earnest, and Mike and Phoebe nodded simultaneously, in perfect sync. It was way past Mary Martha's bedtime and there was going to be hell to pay in the morning, but Rebecca didn't have the heart to break up that scene.

"You knew what you were getting into, right?" she said to Mike that night when they were finally in bed together. Rory had stayed until it was time for Mary Martha to go to sleep, which had been potentially awkward, but Mary Martha had effortlessly solved the dilemma of the tuck-in by having both Rory *and* Mike read her bedtime story. They had begun by alternating pages, a little tentatively, but by the end they were alternating lines and using a variety of outrageous voices and accents, and the laughter of the three of them up there had been audible all through the house. But it was quiet at last, and it was beginning to feel like they were actually home.

Rebecca and Mike had already assumed their best position, in each other's arms with Rebecca's head under Mike's chin and his nose in her hair, and their legs entwined like braided bread.

Mike chest's still smelled, ever so faintly, of coconut. She figured that had one more shower cycle.

"I think I had the basic idea," Mike said. "I must have missed the fine print on the ex-husband with the sledgehammer."

"Rory does this kind of thing once in a while. He once took our car engine apart to save us some money on a valve job and never did get it back together. We took the bus everywhere for about three months and eventually had to sell the car for parts and buy a VW van. Which of course is what he wanted all along." Rebecca shook her head. "What really surprised me was Phoebe. Two years ago—*one* year ago—she would never have let that happen."

"Apparently Mary Martha made her promise—"

"I know, I know. Her hands were tied. It's just not the mother I know." She leaned back slightly to meet his eyes. "You two looked pretty cozy there on the back porch for a while. I don't know whether to be grateful or jealous."

"I adore Phoebe, you know that," Mike said. "She's easy for me, somehow."

"She keeps saying she wishes she were dead. But she says it so cheerfully. Sometimes I think she may just be trying to get a rise out of me."

Mike seemed inclined to dispute that, then smiled and conceded, "That would be Phoebe-like. Though I think there's more to it than sheer orneriness."

"Well, I hate it when she talks like that. It seems to me that it's practically my *job* right now to hate it." She hesitated, then said, "What do *you* two talk about?"

"Not much. It's more like music, what we do now."

"Well maybe I'm just tone-deaf. Because this new hit-or-miss coherence of hers is freaking me out."

"She's okay. Just coming at things from a different angle."

"I hope so," Rebecca said. "It's just so hard, this different woman. It scares me. Half the time when I look at her I just want to cry. It took her five minutes tonight to find the word *redemption*."

"That's not bad," Mike said. "It takes most of us years."

Rebecca laughed and put her head back under his chin. She could feel him breathing her in, as if she were a flower. Their familiar and comforting entwinement felt slightly self-conscious tonight, and it took Rebecca a moment to place her emotion: it was a marriage night, tonight. Not a wedding night, not a honeymoon night. A marriage night. They had come back from a trip together to stacked-up mail and newspapers, survived a mutual social event, dealt with her mother and with friends. They had no running water in the kitchen and were without a working stove. Their refrigerator was in the living room. Their kid had to get up for school in the morning, and Rebecca was already feeling the dread of peeling back the dust-covered sheets of plastic in her studio the next day and getting to the piles of neglected work beneath them. She had never felt more married. This was it. And it felt good. How strange, she thought, to find that such a surprise.

"Welcome home, Mr. Christopher," she murmured into her husband's chest, and she could feel his smile against her forehead.

"Mrs. Christopher," Mike said, "welcome home."

Chapter Six

*Truly I say unto you, If you have done these kindnesses
to any of the lowest of my brethren,
you have done them unto me.*

MATTHEW 25:40

Dear Brother James,

Hello, my friend. It seems like forever since I have written to
you. I think I have even been afraid to write to you, in some ways.
To articulate what I always seem to have to say to you, to speak
truly about my soul and the workings of God in me, seems to lead
me to an abyss of sorts. I peer over the edge, and see the ruinous
fall—from grace, from the life I have hoped for, from everything I
consciously hold dear. There is never a question that it is anything
but God that has led me to that edge, but still I look for a way
around. And look, and look, and finally panic and try to run away.
But in the end every path leads to that abyss. And so I am finally
defeated, as always, into my heedless leap.

I thought I might be done with that stuff. How ridiculous is
that? As if, after a lifetime spent in the desert with the demons and

the dryness and the emptiness of the self, I could suddenly become a civilian in the oasis of normality, a cheerful well-integrated man, a bit sweaty perhaps in the usual humidity, but still a productive member of society. It is much more likely I will run this body into the ground, wreck my life and the lives of those I love, fail in every direction, wreak havoc wherever my fear drives me—until at last I am brought home through sufficient wreckage and the final grace of complete failure to the desert that is everywhere, to the abyss that is my home.

At which point, apparently, I will write to you. You are like a therapist I talk to only after the suicidal urges have passed.

You said in your letter that you hoped I was adjusting well to my new domestic life and thriving in my new world, and while I appreciate the sentiment, I have to say that adjusting too well and thriving too much is one of my greatest fears here. Though there is apparently no danger of that: my job interviews so far have been a series of humiliations. Aside from the paucity—even the bizarreness—of my résumé, I'm afraid I don't come across well when they ask me seven-habits-of-highly-successful-people things like "Where do you see yourself, careerwise, in ten years?" and "What do you feel you bring to the table here?" The truth is, a career just looks like a jail cell to me, and I don't bring shit to the table.

As for my home life ... I feel, as I have felt from the beginning here, utterly blessed and completely terrified. My love for Rebecca is such pure joy; I could live forever in that woman's eyes and never miss a thing. And yet, I feel far from entirely domesticated, and even suspect that the feral element in me is crucial. Jesus wasn't kidding when he said he came bringing not peace, but a sword; nor when he said that anyone who didn't hate his father, mother, wife, and children—yea, and his own life also—could not be his disciple. I took him literally for twenty years, scorning peace and kin and self like a child learning his ABCs with a hammer, and thought in my sterile smugness that my cross was solitude and emptiness; but I can tell you now that to "hate" yourself and family while actually living with them, and loving them, to be free of the world's blind loyalties and compulsive demands while still responding to human particulars with tenderness and compassion, is the real, staggering, almost unbearable cross, and that the steepness of Calvary in actual life often makes the monastery gig look like a downhill stroll with a valet.

I don't mean to denigrate your own vocation, or monastic life in general. God knows, if I had managed to learn to love my enemy in Abbot Hackley, they'd be doing the research for my beatification by now. In many ways this is a second marriage for me, after a decades-long failure of monumental proportions. In the end, we have to do both our hating and our loving right where we are, carrying the cross we're given up the hill in front of us; and Jesus himself fell three times on the way up. So I guess we'll both just keep on trucking. And God help us both.

Love,
Mike

•   •   •

ut of the depths have I cried unto thee, O Lord.

      It was strange to climb, to go *up* to pray. Prayer had felt like a place he sank into, a depth, for such a long time that he could only marvel at the old days when it had felt like a path upward, when he had read Merton's *Ascent to Truth* and longed to climb the holy mountain, to labor upward toward the heights of contemplation by the steepest possible route. It had all seemed so straightforward then. But that kind of zeal and pro-grammatic patness just felt embarrassing after a while; the real ascent to truth eventually destroyed all the ways you'd hope to rise, and you were well rid of them. But here he was nonetheless, climbing a ladder every morning in the dark.

The wooden steps creaked, but all the oil in the world didn't seem to help that. Rebecca and Mary Martha had both assured him that they never heard the noise, that they slept right through it, but it still sounded painfully loud in the house's predawn silence. It would have been so much easier—quieter, simpler, and certainly less arduous—to just sit in the living room, on the far side of the couch, as he had for several months, or even in the corner of the bedroom, where he had prayed when he and Rebecca first got together. He knew that Rebecca was uneasy with the whole attic thing. She took it personally, as a bad com-mentary on their life somehow, and felt that he was moving away, despite his best efforts to reassure her.

Mike would have liked to accommodate her in that. It shouldn't matter, ideally speaking, *where,* or even when, he prayed.

All the world was the temple of the Lord, and every moment was
as holy as every other. But the attic in the predawn just felt better.
It felt like getting out of the traffic somehow. No doubt a sufficiently centered person could commune with God in any old
spot, but he just wasn't that guy. And, he reminded himself often,
even Jesus had taken himself off into the hills sometimes to escape
the crowds and pray alone.

Maybe he was a little defensive about it all.

I wait for the Lord, my soul doth wait, and in his word do I hope.

At the top of the ladder, the attic's darkness was absolute.
Mike picked up the flashlight he always left at the entry and
made his way, along the plywood walkway he had laid across the
beams, to the back wall. In the early days up here he had sat near
the ladder, but he'd gradually worked his way west, as if moved by
some sort of gravity. He eventually wanted to put a window in
the wall he'd ended up in front of, which made almost no sense
at all. He was sitting here with his eyes closed, after all. In the
dark.

His prayer mat was spread before the small altar he'd set up.
Mike lit the single votive candle there, sat down, and got to it.

*My soul waiteth for the Lord more than they that watch for morn-
ing: I say, more than they that watch for the morning.*

In the kitchen, Mike turned on the first light of the day and
started a pot of coffee. While it percolated, he washed the
last of the previous evening's dishes in the tiny bathroom

sink—Rory, despite his best efforts, had not been able to restore normal plumbing to the kitchen yet—went over Mary Martha's math and spelling homework, which she always left on the kitchen table, and went out to the living room to check the refrigerator for breakfast milk and lunch fixings. The coffee was ready by then, and he poured himself a cup. It was just after 6:00 AM; in the monastery, the private masses said by the monks during lauds would be giving way now to *lectio divina,* a period of sacred reading, before prime rang and they gathered to sing the conventual mass. Here, Mike took down the copy of the Bible and a volume of poems by Rumi that he kept on top of the refrigerator. He still felt the small thrill of reading the Islamic mystic without compunction; it had always driven Abbot Hackley a little nuts when he read Rumi during the *lectio.* One more of the unforeseen joys of spiritual catastrophe. Rebecca, he knew, had no problem with Rumi but was actually a little uneasy with a Bible on top of the fridge. You never quite got used to ironies like that.

He read quietly for a time, before a movement in the doorway caught his eye. Mike looked up and found Mary Martha standing there.

"Oh!" he said. "Good morning, sweet pea."

"Good morning."

"Are you all right?" he asked, hoping she hadn't had a bad dream or something. Mary Martha, who had not even been aware that the attic existed until Mike had started going up there, had gone through a period of concern about the attic monsters coming down the ladder during the night. One more of the ironies of the life of prayer: you opened your inner doors to the Mystery, and your kid had to deal with the demons too. That wasn't something you found in *The Cloud of Unknowing*. No amount of reassurance or guided tours of the attic during the day to demonstrate its unpopulated harmlessness had helped; Mary Martha had not relaxed until Mike had convinced her that he knew all the good monsters up there, and that the good monsters ate the bad monsters. Even now, a huge purple Puff the Magic Dragon stood guard at Mary Martha's bedroom door every night, just in case a bad monster made it down to the domestic level. Puff, thank God, was always hungry; bad monsters were like chocolate to him.

"I'm fine," Mary Martha said. She lingered in the doorway— shyly, Mike thought, which was unusual between them, as Mary Martha had felt free and easy with him pretty much from the beginning.

"You're up early," he said.

"So are you," she noted, a little defensively, as if to say she had every right to be up now too. Mike realized that she was already dressed, everything buttoned down, zipped up, and otherwise in place except her flopping shoelaces.

"So we're up together," he conceded. "Do you want some cereal?"

"I would like some tea," Mary Martha said, quite formally. "Please."

This too was unprecedented, but Mike thought he understood: matching his coffee. Cups of hot liquid, one each. He said, throwing in a touch of an English accent, "Certainly, miss, coming right up. Won't you have a seat?"

Mary Martha gave him the first hint of a smile and crossed to the table. He got the kettle going, and while it heated he came back and knelt before her chair to tie her shoes. Mary Martha's shirt buttons were skewed, he noted, one hole too high per button. He wrestled briefly with the dilemma of whether to fix them or not and decided to let it go. He already understood that as a parent he tended to err on the side of letting the kid make as many of her own mistakes as possible. The usual morning dressing routine involved Rebecca; she and Mary Martha allotted fifteen minutes, post-Cheerios, for a protracted closet meditation, the discussion of fashion choices, and all manner of subtlety and fastidiousness. But clearly this was not a usual morning.

"I can do that," Mary Martha said, of the shoelaces. "I just forgot."

"Of course," Mike said, not believing her for a second. But he leaned back obligingly while Mary Martha leaned forward, and watched as she took hold of the laces. To his surprise, she looped the ear deftly, then chased the bunny around the garden, into the burrow, and out the other side. Zip, boom, bam, done.

"Was that the Bunny?" Mike said. He felt like he'd missed a turn somewhere. He was pretty sure he'd seen Mary Martha make a total mess of the whole laces thing with Phoebe the day before, during one of their marathon grandmother-granddaughter shoe-tying seminars.

"The Rabbit." Mary Martha tied the other shoe with similar ease.

"You've been holding out on me," Mike said, a little accusingly.

Mary Martha shrugged. "I go slow for Gran-Gran sometimes," she said. "I don't want her to feel bad."

Mike felt his eyes sting. "That's very gracious of you," he said, instead of crying, and straightened to take his seat beside her.

"Do we need to go over your homework?" he asked.

"No."

"Really? How do you spell *train?*"

"Train," Mary Martha said. "T-r-a-i-n. Train."

"What is seven plus four?"

"Eleven."

Mike pretended to count on his own fingers, and looked baffled when he ran out of them at ten. "How did you *do* that?"

Mary Martha rewarded him with the second smile of the day. "It's easy, silly."

"Easy for some people."

"Seven *minus* four is three," she said.

The kettle gave a first tentative tweet, and Mike hurried to catch it before it whistled and woke up Rebecca.

"What kind of tea do you like?" he asked, opening the cupboard. New territory here, for sure. "We've got chamomile, peppermint—"

"Lipton's, please," Mary Martha said.

Mike hesitated. There was in fact a box of orange pekoe there among all the herbal teas, but he wasn't sure of the house policy. He really didn't like undermining the sometimes arcane disciplines and regulations Rebecca tried to enforce, but he also hated to seem gun-shy or letter of the law.

"You know that has caffeine in it," he said, by way of compromise.

"Not as much as coffee," Mary Martha pointed out.

"Well—"

"Coke has caffeine," Mary Martha persisted. "Mountain *Dew* has caffeine."

This was true. The kid knew more about caffeine than he did. Mike pulled out a Lipton's bag and dropped it into her Pikachu mug.

"Cream and sugar, Miss?"

"Cream?"

"A lot of people like cream in their coffee or tea. Your mom does."

"Do you?"

"Just a dollop."

"A 'dollop'?"

"Dollop," Mike said. "D-o-l-l-o-p. Dollop. A dollop is a doll-sized plollop."

"Okay," Mary Martha said dubiously, clearly resigning herself to the mysteries of adult sophistication; and then, after he had gone out to the living room and come back with the carton from the refrigerator, "That's just *milk.*"

"We call it cream when we're being prim and proper about hot drinks."

"Oh."

He brought her the steaming mug and sat down at the table with her. Mary Martha stirred in a tremendous spoonful of sugar, then sat back.

"You have to let it steep," she said.

"Absolutely. It's crucial."

They sat quietly for a moment. Mike snuck a glance at the clock, then let it go. He was already figuring he would miss the morning mass today. This was way more fun. But Mary Martha caught his look and said, "Is it time to go yet?"

"To church?" She nodded. "There's still a few minutes. But I'd much rather stay here with you, if you—"

"Actually," Mary Martha said, "I want to go with you."

Shit, Mike thought. Her tone had the same formal— rehearsed, he understood now— inflection with which she had asked for tea. He realized that he was delighted, in a deep way, but the situation seemed overwhelmingly complex. Aside from the fact that he was already letting Mary Martha have caffeine and walk around with her shirt buttoned wrong, he had long understood that Rebecca was wary of him "laying a Catholicism thing" on her daughter. One of the trickiest phases of their relationship had come while Phoebe was in the hospital the previous autumn, after her stroke, and Mike had taken Mary Martha several times to light prayer candles for her grandmother. Rebecca had relented on that, eventually, or at least had cut her losses; but Mike had pretty much bent over backward since to avoid similar conflicts.

"Really?" he said now, feeling stupid.

"Yes," Mary Martha said firmly.

He'd seen her act the same way about buckling her own seat belt, sharpening her own pencil, and scooping out the insides of her own pumpkins at Halloween. At least it was clear now what all this early morning activity was about.

"All right, then," Mike said, "let's fix your buttons."

I n the dim narthex of St. Jude's, Mary Martha dipped her fingers into the font of holy water and crossed herself studiously. She'd learned the ritual during the lighting-candles-for-Phoebe period, though Mike had taught her the movements as his grandfather had first taught him—glasses, belt buckle, watch, wallet—so that Mary Martha's devotional motions looked more like an old man checking himself to be sure he was together before leaving the house. If this church thing went much further, Mike knew, he was going to have to introduce her to the Father, Son, and Holy Ghost—and then, he realized, explain to her also somehow that the Holy Ghost was now the Holy Spirit. He could just picture Mary Martha earnestly relaying all that theology to Rebecca.

There seemed no way around it. Rock, hard place. He was screwed.

They paused at the bank of candles beneath the statue of the

Virgin, whom Mike had introduced to Mary Martha as Mary, as he was loath to begin his stepdaughter's sex education with the notion of the Immaculate Conception. Mary Martha took one of the long tapers with a seasoned if self-conscious air, lit a candle, and knelt briefly before the shrine with her eyes fiercely closed. She never said what she was lighting the candles for; she seemed to feel that birthday-candle wish etiquette applied and that the prayer would not come true if she said what it was.

Mike led them to his usual row, as far back in the tiers of pews as possible without getting ostentatious about it. Any farther back and people would have had to wonder if he was a serial killer or something; any closer and he'd have felt compelled to interact like a decent human being with his fellow worshippers. The morning mass crowd was the usual dozen or so elderly solitaries, borderline eccentrics, and earnest salt-of-the-earth people who got straight on the N-Judah train after mass to go to work. Mike eased the kneeler down and knelt, and Mary Martha mirrored him, folding her small hands atop the pew. An angel. An innocent. An unwritten scripture.

God help me, Mike thought. God. Help. Me.

"Where *is* everybody?" Mary Martha whispered.

"This is pretty much it," Mike whispered back.

"Then why are there so many seats?"

"For Sundays. Most people only come on Sunday."

Mary Martha took this in and was silent for a long moment. Then she leaned over again and said, "Can God hear us if we whisper?"

Mike hesitated. He was tempted to start straight in on the mythico-metaphorical nature of God's ears. The true answer seemed to him to be that one child's earnest whisper was probably worth a thousand generations of proper church behavior. The book answer, of course, was, Yes, sweetheart, God hears everything, with some kind of asterisk about His understanding and mercy. But Mike recalled how much God as divine hall monitor had terrified him as a child of Mary Martha's age. The nuns who had taught him the Baltimore Catechism had emphasized that his thoughts were an open book to God. He'd felt for years like his head was caught in a constant X-ray beam, his every wide-eyed inner lapse a deer in the headlights of the Lord.

Still, there was no way around certain basics. Mike said, opting for the asterisk, "Yes, but he's very discreet."

"What's discreet?"

The bell rang, a mercy. Mike stood, with Mary Martha a beat behind, and the priest and altar boy hustled onto the altar from offstage and got to it.

"In the name of the Father, and of the Son, and of the Holy Spirit."

"Amen."

"The Lord be with you."

"And also with you."

Mike realized that Mary Martha didn't have a script. He took a missal from the rack on the pew back and opened it to the introductory rites. By the time he had found the right page, they were already through the Kyrie. The morning mass was a very wham-bam-thank-you-ma'am affair, like framing work in carpentry, just drive the fundamental nails, knock the boards together, and get the walls up. They left the interior decoration and finish work for Sundays.

He held the book open in front of them anyway, on principle. Mary Martha bent over it attentively. The text seemed tiny, gray, and impossibly close, and Mike knew how fast this little girl could read right now anyway. When he'd been Mary Martha's age, they'd still been saying the mass in Latin, and he remembered waiting, waiting, waiting through the incomprehensible mumble of the adults' words for the moments when he could say "Amen." He'd keyed, desperately and usually unsuccessfully, on certain words he could pick out of the Latin stew like carrot chunks; he'd been so afraid that God thought he was screwing up.

The mass right now might as well still be in Latin as far as Mary Martha was concerned. Even moving his fingertip under the words to help her follow was a stretch; and Mike finally bent close to her ear and whispered, to the tempo of the prayer in progress, "Blahblah, blah blahblah, blah blah ... three, two, one, *Amen.*"

Mary Martha giggled. The congregation sat for the Liturgy of the Word, and an earnest woman in sneakers and sweatpants, with hair that seemed cemented into shape, approached the lectern for the reading from the Old Testament. Mike had hoped for some kind of slam-dunk scripture, love and light and mercy, today of all days, but it was the twelfth Wednesday in Ordinary

Time, God's sense of humor had hit the ground running this morning, and the first reading was from Lamentations 2.

The Lord hath purposed to destroy the wall of the daughter of Zion: He hath stretched out a line; He hath not withdrawn His hand from destroying: therefore He made the rampart and the wall to lament; they languished together.

Mary Martha sat with her hands in her lap, wide-eyed. Mike hoped she wasn't really following as closely as it looked like she was. How do you spell divine retribution, sweetheart? Capital D...

Her gates are sunk into the ground; He hath destroyed and broken her bars. Her king and her princes are among the Gentiles; the law is no more; her prophets also find no vision from the Lord.

God, Mike thought again. Help. Me.

Arise, cry out in the night: in the beginning of the watches pour out thine heart like water before the face of the Lord: lift up thy hands toward Him for the life of thy young children, that faint for hunger in the top of every street.

The lector looked up solemnly, her hair an unmoving testament, and intoned, "This is the Word of the Lord."

"Thanks be to God," Mike said resignedly, with the rest of the congregation. He'd already looked ahead; the Epistle was even worse.

R ebecca woke, as she almost always did now, to the creak, crunch, and thump of the attic stairs folding up and the trapdoor swinging back into the ceiling. Mike's little morning cleanup. He was skittish and self-conscious about the mechanics of his attic access, as if his prayer life were something akin to alcoholism and this morning ritual amounted to trying to get the empty bottles into the trash can quietly. His attempts to keep the noisy ladder's ups and downs off the radar screen had, of course, only made them weirdly central. Aside from the prolonged phase of getting Mary Martha calmed down about the monster traffic, the ladder going up when Mike got back from morning mass had come to be like a rooster crowing for Rebecca, and she suspected it was the same for her daughter. Shutting those monsters in.

Oh, well, she thought now. It could be worse. Rory usually hadn't even bothered to clean up after his own bad habits. When Mary Martha had been a toddler, Rebecca had always circled through the house before her daughter woke, to make sure the remains of the previous night's activities had been disposed of. She'd once caught a two-year-old Mary Martha about to eat the butt end of a joint left on the coffee table. The kid had known what a roach clip was before she'd known what a hair clip was. At least Mike's intemperance left no edible residues.

The bedroom door eased open, a palpable change in the air rather than a noise. Mike had developed some sort of soundless technique for turning the knob, as if the extra several seconds of sleep such consideration might afford Rebecca mattered, but she could always feel the draft from the hall. The deal was, Mike slipped in with coffee for her and woke her with a kiss. Rebecca kept her eyes closed as he entered, to perpetuate the illusion of slumber undisturbed by any reality other than her lover's arrival. They had their own little off-Broadway reenactment of *Sleeping Beauty* going every morning here. The elaborate ritual was completely over-the-top, but they both loved it.

It always took Mike longer to cross the room than seemed possible, but Rebecca knew he was taking his clothes off somehow en route. She wondered how he did it with the coffee in his hand, because there was no place to set the mug down between the door and the bed, but she'd never peeked at the process, preferring to enjoy the slightly mysterious touch of magic it lent. Prince Charming as an amazingly silent and somewhat acrobatic stripper.

She felt rather than heard his presence beside her, and smelled the coffee as the mug was eased onto its coaster on the bedside table; and at last Mike slipped beneath the quilt and his arms found the perfect way around her, in the true daily miracle, and the length of his body molded itself to her nakedness. His lips

touched her face, just beside her nose, a kiss like a butterfly landing, and she felt his warmth and the slight sandpaper scrape of his
unshaved early morning beard and heard the gentle flux of his
breath as he breathed her in. He liked her smell, he always said.
No one had ever liked her smell before.

She liked his smell too. Thank God.

"Mmm," she murmured, stirring, turning toward him.

"Mmm-hmm," Mike said.

They lay quietly in each other's arms. It would be somewhere between 6:58 and 7:03, Rebecca knew, which meant they
had between seventeen and twenty-two minutes until Mary
Martha's alarm went off. Sometimes they went the whole twenty-
some minutes without saying a coherent word. She liked that
best.

To hell with meditation, she thought. Give me this. Love
mumbling into love, a warmth that held the world at bay, with
nowhere to go and nothing to do but love and mumble.
Rebecca wondered if that was terrible, if it made her a shallow
person. She didn't particularly want to be good, wise, or even
articulate; she didn't really want to accomplish a damn thing in
the world beyond keeping her child happy and alive. She just
wanted this man's arms around her. It was so easy to lose sight
of that during the hectic days of doing this and that, of being
this necessary person or that one. She just wanted her body
entwined with the body of this guy who liked her smell.

"You smell like cookies," she said.

"Well, we stopped at the bakery."

Rebecca registered the caution in his tone before she'd fully digested the meaning of the sentence. She opened her eyes and found Mike looking at her, his eyebrows slightly up, transparently hoping she would take this well.

"'We,'" she said.

"Mary Martha wanted to go to mass with me this morning." And, as Rebecca said nothing, "There was no stopping her, I swear."

It made her furious that he expected her to be upset, which was completely unreasonable, because she knew perfectly well she'd given him plenty of cause to expect her to be upset. It wasn't that she was opposed to God, per se. She just didn't want His damn church screwing with her daughter's head.

Rebecca sat up and reached for her coffee, trying to buy some time for herself to calm down, and noted that the clock read 7:17, which meant they had precisely three minutes to process this.

She sipped the coffee and it was cold. Of course it was cold, it was symbolic, for God's sake. This precious period before the world kicked in was not about the coffee being the right temperature. But if the world was going to kick in this early, she wanted her coffee hot.

"I hope you at least bought me a cinnamon scone," she said.

"They were out of scones. I got you a muffin."

"How the hell could a bakery be out of scones at seven in the morning?"

"It's that little Chinese place at the corner of Fortieth. There's an emphasis on deep-fried things and lots of glaze."

"The Chinese have never understood the importance of baking," Rebecca said.

They were silent for a moment, mutually assessing the state of the art. She could feel Mike hoping she would keep it light. She was hoping that herself.

"What kind of muffin?" she asked at last.

"I was going to get some kind of apple-bran thing, but Mary Martha said you liked blueberry."

"Or cranberry," Rebecca conceded. "White flour. Life is too short for bran."

"Live and learn," Mike said. She could feel his tentative relief, which only made it harder to be decent. They were a long way from through this thing.

In the kitchen, Mary Martha was already dressed—in yesterday's clothes, Rebecca noted. It was probably too much to expect a seven-year-old to get her wardrobe together by herself before dawn, but it was all Rebecca could do to bite back a comment. Her daughter was sitting at the table with a bowl of Cheerios and the remnants of some kind of gigantic pastry that Rebecca didn't recognize. There was already a small plate set up at the spot beside her, with Rebecca's muffin on it, and a napkin, plastic knife, and pat of butter from the bakery laid neatly beside it. Rebecca wondered whether that had been Mike's touch or Mary Martha's. Both of them were treating her like a bomb that might go off.

She did not want to be that person. She would not be that person.

"What *is* that?" she asked her daughter, of the pastry, as she sat down beside her.

"A panda's foot."

"A *panda's* foot. Wow. I never heard of a panda's foot before."

"A bear claw," Mike translated quietly from the counter, where he was refilling her coffee mug. "Chinese. Bear claw. So, a panda."

She caught his look, inviting her to share their usual delight in the working of Mary Martha's brain. The shameless bastard.

Rebecca reached for her muffin. Mike delivered the fresh coffee and went back to fix a cup for himself. Mary Martha reached for the milk carton and said, with a trace of an English accent, "Cream, Miss?"

"Please," Rebecca said, a little unnerved. She watched her daughter pour enough milk into the coffee to drown any chance of it still being warm. If she was going to tolerate this sudden influx of God into their lives before breakfast, she needed hot coffee. Needed it badly. But that appeared beyond reach.

"I hear you went to church this morning," she said to Mary Martha.

"Uh-huh."

"How was it?"

"Good," Mary Martha said.

"Did you learn any new, uh, prayers?"

Mike came back to the table and sat down with his own perfectly hot coffee. Mary Martha gave him a conspiratorial glance, and he smiled and shrugged a kind of permission. She turned back to Rebecca and recited, deadpan, "Blahblahblah, blahblah blah, blah blah blah."

"Three, two, one—" Mike said, and the two of them chorused, "Amen," and giggled.

Rebecca realized that she had been half hoping Mary Martha would come up with something over-the-top, something so religiously wacko and patently destructive to her tender little psyche that the wrongheadedness of this would be obvious to all of them and they could get on with their secular lives in the fallen world. But clearly Mike was on the case, and it was probably too much to hope for the institution to show its colors so neatly on first encounter. If this kept up, though, she might have to hire a nun with a stick, to get her daughter up to speed on Catholicism as she knew it.

The muffin, at least, was delicious.

"Cream, Sir?" Mary Martha asked Mike.

"Just a dollop, please."

"A dollop is a doll-sized plollop," Mary Martha informed Rebecca, as she wrecked Mike's coffee too. But he seemed cheerful enough about it.

"How about that," Rebecca said.

•   •   •

When Mary Martha finally finished her Cheerios and went upstairs to brush her teeth, Rebecca took her coffee straight to the microwave, set the machine on three minutes, and punched the button hard.

"I know, I know," Mike said.

"Do you, now?"

"Let's say I have an inkling."

"A little dollop of Catholicism, huh?"

"At least she'll have something to work with when she rebels against it all in her teens and embraces Buddhism."

Rebecca wanted to ask Mike how he'd gotten Mary Martha out of bed that early in the first place, as her daughter was generally even less of a morning person than Rebecca herself, but she couldn't find a tone in her head for the question that wouldn't sound overly aggressive. They were both trying so hard, she didn't want to fire the first shot. Instead, she opened the microwave and stuck her finger into her coffee, which wasn't even lukewarm yet. She put it back in the machine and shut the door firmly. It came across sounding like a slam.

Mike, apparently taking the door as commentary, said defensively, "A lot of people have survived Catholic childhoods and gone on to lead normal, productive lives." And, with a rueful smile, as Rebecca said nothing, "Present company excepted, of course."

"I'm prepared to stipulate that I may be a little insane about this."

He looked genuinely surprised. "I meant *me*."

"Oh," Rebecca said. "Well, then, I take it back."

The microwave roared on. No doubt she was being fatally irradiated, standing here.

Mike confided, with an air of concession, "The Old Testament reading was from Lamentations."

"I'm not up to speed on the scriptural subtleties here, buddy."

"Let's just say it made your point."

Rebecca crossed back to the table and sat down. A peace offering.

"It was the good priest, at least," Mike said, apparently still determined to process this with her as if they were on the same team.

"The gay one or the Vietnamese guy?"

"The gay one. He said a few words to us after the mass, very pleasant. Mary Martha likes him."

"Have you told her yet that she can't *be* a priest? Or gay, for that matter?"

"I thought I'd hold off on the critique of patriarchy and sexuality in Western civilization until second semester."

They were silent a moment, as people who had almost stepped off a curb might be silent after a bus had roared by.

"Jesus, Mike," Rebecca said at last.

"Yeah." He smiled. "Literally."

"I suppose I should have seen this coming."

"You did see it coming. We both did. And neither of us particularly wanted it."

"Bullshit. You're happy as a clam."

"A very conflicted clam." She smiled, almost grudgingly, at the image. Mike smiled back and said as mildly as a human being possibly could, "I'm betting your coffee is hot enough by now."

Rebecca shrugged and let the microwave roar on. She wasn't prepared to give away the store here. There were only so many things she was going to let him be not wrong about on a morning like this.

"Those are yesterday's clothes she's wearing, you know," she noted, because she could.

"At least we got the buttons right.... Did you know that she can tie her own shoes now? I mean, like a pro?"

"Since when?"

"God knows," Mike said. "It must have come together for her while we were in Hawaii. She sure nailed it this morning, two flips and a twist, and stuck the landing."

"I saw her yesterday—"

"Me too," Mike said. "But she's been bluffing." He hesitated, then said, "She told me she goes slow for Phoebe. So she won't feel bad."

Rebecca's eyes filled with quick tears. Mike met her look in acknowledgment, *that's our girl,* and then stood up and said, "I guess I'd better get up there and make sure she's not setting up a secret shrine to the Sacred Heart or something."

"Or something," Rebecca agreed, brushing her eye with the back of her hand; and as he bent to kiss her, "I still hate you, you know. Just so we're clear."

"I hate you too, sweetheart," her husband said. His lips touched hers, and they held the kiss for a moment.

"She wants to go on Sunday too," he said as he straightened, and fled.

As soon as he was out of the room, Rebecca jumped up and hurried to the microwave, but her coffee had already boiled away, explosively, leaving the inside of the machine dripping gory brown like the aftermath of some kind of caffeine massacre. There was still half a cup of oily, acidic residue puddled in the carafe, but she just dumped it and put some fresh grounds into a clean filter. If this kept up she was going to have to get Mike to at least start a new pot of coffee in the morning when he got back from complicating their daughter's life with God. And, Rebecca vowed to herself, the next chance she had, she was going to teach that kid what a dollop really was.

Later, when Mike took Mary Martha to the bus stop, Rebecca went upstairs to her daughter's room. Sure enough, Mary Martha had somehow managed to set her alarm clock herself, for 5:59. It was a pretty impressive bit of technological initiative for a seven-year-old, and Rebecca realized that she was relieved she hadn't jumped all over Mike about that, at least. It looked like this was something she was probably going to have to live with.

Chapter Seven

Get up and walk. Your sins are forgiven.

MARK 2

Dear Brother James,

 Thank you for your letter, and especially for the update on *Abbot Hackley's condition. The swirl of monastic politics, the posturing and positioning over his succession, is inevitable, I suppose, but no less disgusting for that. I am truly sorry to hear that the chemotherapy did not lead to more improvement, but it does seem that the abbot's state of mind is good and his soul is increasingly at peace. Apparently all he had to do, to appreciate the contemplative side of the monastic life, was begin to die. (It is true of all of us, I suppose.) May he finish the job as beautifully, with God's grace.*

 After our long combat over the balance of the active and the contemplative lives, I hope Abbot Hackley in his belated contemplative peace enjoys the irony of my own tilt into involvement in the world. Although I am singularly ineffectual in my activities. The only really obvious thing I do these days, aside from spending a lot of time sitting around drinking tea with Phoebe, is teach Mary Martha's first communion class on Sunday mornings. Rebecca seems more or less reconciled to her daughter eventually receiving the sacrament; I think she is resigned to the notion that Catholicism may just skip a generation sometimes, like male-pattern baldness or hemophilia.

The classes themselves are a hoot. What do you say to a six- or seven-year-old about the meaning of the Eucharist? Before he was given up to death, a death he freely accepted, he took bread, and gave You thanks. He broke the bread, and gave it to his disciples, saying, Take this, all of you, and eat it: this is my body, which will be given up for you. *That we are fed by God, with God? That Jesus had to be broken, like the bread, to make us whole? That we are made one with Him, and with all believers, through this shared meal that, unfathomably, is Him? The church pastor, who is sort of an old-school jerk, insists that we make the sacrifice real for the kids by teaching them a gruesome version of the stations of the cross, and he and I have already come close to real trouble with each other a couple of times. I find, though, that it is easier now for me to see past the crap—these children in front of me are going to be introduced to God one way or another, whether I blow up at Father Merkle and storm out or not—and it is a real motivation for me to dig deeper for patience.*

And so I steer with the skid of the curriculum, and do what I can to keep it solemn without getting gory, true without getting intricate, and suffused with love without getting foofy. It is a dauntingly difficult and delicate balance, and there is no way around the fact that for a child of that age, all this amounts to a sort of bait and switch anyway. With this first communion they are beginning a

lifetime diet of a love so deep that, God willing, they will be strong
enough to just keep walking into it when they realize that the torn
and broken body, streaming with blood, nailed to that splintered
wood on all those fearful icons, really is their own as well, that Love
really does go through that death, and the Word through that
suffering flesh, in order to be made real in this terrible world. There
is no warning them, much as I would like to; and certainly there is
no preparing them to suffer it by the book, much as Merkle would
like to. I feel like a con man, sometimes.

Perhaps in compensation for my guilt at that, and as a penance
of sorts for so frankly subverting Father Merkle's maniacal agenda, I
have been teaching the kids a modified form of contemplation: they
say "Hello, God," in their hearts and listen quietly and silently for
an answer that is not words. I cannot communicate to you the sense
of awe that arises from the twenty seconds those seven-year-olds are
able to be quiet before they begin to stir and titter. God knows what
God is giving them, but I cannot help but believe that those twenty
seconds of silence are the better part of my so-called ministry.

The job hunt continues worse than futile, a series of small
humiliations and exercises in absurdity. It is probably only a matter
of time before I go back to cooking hamburgers. I had gotten a bit
ahead on money during my stint at McDonald's, but that cushion is
pretty much gone now and I definitely feel the pressure of being so
nonproductive, economically. Rebecca has been wonderfully patient
and supportive, but I have to step up somehow.

I really don't see how anyone finds time to earn a living,
frankly. I mean, when do they pray? By the time you've got the

most minimal meditation done, and found a little quality time with your loved ones, and taken a shower, there really doesn't seem to be a moment left in the day.

Love,
Mike

The world had stopped, and Phoebe waited, because the world whirled on. The stopping wasn't something you did, and the whirling wasn't something you could stop. It was the dawn of the last day, which went on forever, and the sleepless night of time, and the hour of our death, amen. It was darkness everywhere and always, and it was always bright, and the wind beat at the windows. The storm was grief over everything that love had failed to do; and when you finally knew that love had never had anything to do but spend itself as love, you turned somehow into the nothing that love did, and the wind blew through you as peace, and the storm was soft as a baby's grip.

And here he was again, the one for her daughter. One of the last ones she could see, barely blurred at all. She wondered how he stayed in focus, moving through the storm like that.

"Good morning, Phoebe."

"Is it morning again?"

"Like clockwork," Mike said. "Would you like some tea?"

"If that's what's on the schedule."

Mike ran some water into the kettle, took it to the stove and brought up the flame, then came back and sat down at the table with her.

"You're up early today," he said.

"I may have forgotten to sleep," Phoebe said. "Is that terribly important?"

"Right up there with eating."

"Points off, I guess," Phoebe said. "My bad."

"No big deal. Nobody's really keeping score."

"Liar," Phoebe said, and was pleased when he laughed. Because everyone was keeping score, of course. It kept their minds off the storm until the roof blew off. Her mother and father used to give her pennies when she was good. Her grandmother gave her nickels with buffalo on them, and those dimes they had before Roosevelt. And so you lived your life that way, piling up penny payoffs for good deeds, with the occasional nickel-and-dime bonus, trained trick by trick into the performance of decency, until it became the only way you could see the world, as if truth and love were a bank account and the game was to accumulate a hefty balance. And in the end you had this mass of cold dirty metal that you spent most of your energy hauling around and protecting, and just about the time you broke down under the weight of it, you realized that God didn't care a bit what you'd piled up, and never had, He only cared what you'd spent.

But there was no one to say this to, and no comfort in the telling, for the living or the dead. The words turned razor edged in the wind and left an aftertaste like blood or smoke. And who spoke, anyway, and who heard? The voices only burned in ears that could bear the hurt.

Something screamed, a rising shriek, a voice broken by the storm into pure keening, a soul readied at last by despair for salvation, and Mike rose and went to the stove to turn off the flame beneath the kettle and pour the water over their tea bags in the mugs.

"How *do* you know what to do?" Phoebe asked, impressed.

Mike shrugged modestly. "I just wait for the whistle and get to it."

"God doesn't tell you?"

Mike laughed. "God doesn't tell me shit."

"Ah, He tells me everything now," Phoebe said. "But not a word about what to do."

"Honey?" Mike asked, bringing the mugs to the table.

"Sweetheart," Phoebe echoed fondly, and watched as he upended the little bear and squeezed the sweet gold from it. He was so good, she thought, amid the complexities of it all. He really was the most amazing man.

"I should give you a penny," she said.

"No need to tip," Mike said. "I'm in it for the company I keep."

• • •

Rebecca was trying to find an extension cord that would make it from the living room to her printer in the dining room, but the only extension cords long enough to do the job were already hooked up to the refrigerator. It seemed to be coming down to a choice between printing her graphics and having unsoured milk. Rory had a day off from work and was using it to take a determined run at getting the kitchen finished, which was wonderful in principle, but he was doing something complicated and Rory-esque with the fuse box and there was no power in the kitchen. This was not that big a deal, since they had not used the kitchen seriously for weeks now except for storage and transit, but it also meant there was no power in the outlets on the kitchen side of Rebecca's studio-cum–dining room, and her fax machine, printer, and scanner had been useless all morning. She was working on a deadline and needed the printer badly. She would need the fax machine badly once she had used the printer. She had needed the scanner since yesterday, but that was arguably for work she should have done last week and so not entirely Rory's fault.

It would also have been nice to have light, but the ceiling bulb was out too and she was working from a single lamp plugged into the overloaded outlet on the room's street side. Rory had been assuring her for the last hour that it would only be five more minutes until the power was restored, but it had been twenty minutes since he had zipped through for the last reassurance before disappearing into the basement again with a different screwdriver, and during that time the only thing that had happened was that half of the power upstairs had gone off too.

Rebecca had a sense of having regressed to a circle of hell from the previous decade. Her ex's nonchalant incompetence and the constant implication that she was taking everything too seriously were all too familiar, and it made her want to kill him just as it always had. Rory was now a decent citizen and even, arguably, a pretty good father, but he was still a maddening piece of work.

Ironic, Rebecca thought, considering her options: definitely ironic, to kill him now, after all these years. But never more satisfying.

Instead, she unplugged the refrigerator and took the precious line to get the printer up. The milk would have to take its chances.

The phone rang while the machine was still going through its intricate warm-up beeps and rumbles. She noted the number on the caller ID and considered just letting it ring but finally picked up.

"I hate to seem like a nag—" Jeff Burgess said.

"I've got the images on my screen. I just have to print them."

"That's what you said fifteen minutes ago. I've got three guys from Marzipan sitting in the meeting room on their second cups of coffee."

"Have you given them any candy?"

"For God's sake, Becca—"

"Sorry. But who names a tech company after a confection?"

"You have the right to make jokes as soon as you fax the presentation."

The printer had calmed down and was online now. Rebecca hit the file's "Print All" button. There was an unnerving pause from across the room; it would take a minute or two for the large file to get going. She said, "I'm sorry, the power has been out here all morning. They're doing some, uh, repairs."

"Couldn't they have waited until you had this done?"

Rebecca considered going into the domestic details, then realized that would be nuts. Jeff had been her boss during her years at Utopian Images, a graphics company downtown that Jeff had begun almost a decade earlier mainly to employ himself and his artist friends and to make some good-karma income. It had been a very hip and laid-back scene for years, with a lot of soft deadlines, after-hours parties, and an ongoing intraoffice sexual soap opera, but at some point they had actually started making money and economic realism in a corporate world had set in. There had been a time when Rebecca could have explained to Jeff that this could be the only chance in the next several months for her ex-husband to get their kitchen working again, that Mary Martha hadn't had a hot meal sitting down since May, and that Rebecca had been spending many of the hours she should have been spending on this crucial project with her increasingly demented mother discussing the planting schedule in a garden where everything died within two weeks, but those days were long gone. Most of the old crew of hippies and dopers had kids and mortgages now, and Utopian Images had a dress code, a good health plan, and accounts with the electric company, Bank of America, and Bechtel. Jeff still wore only the most outrageous Jerry Garcia ties, but he had a haircut like a marine and a second house in the mountains.

The printer hiccuped and ground its gears briefly, then began at last to spew the sheets. The artwork for this job seemed hideous to Rebecca, a series of cloyingly sweet images. But apparently that was what they wanted at Marzipan.

"We have liftoff—" Rebecca said, just as all the power in the house went out.

"Thank God," Jeff replied, mercifully oblivious to the new development.

"Yeah." The printer had frozen with the first sheet half printed. Rebecca noted that everything had come out in a vague bluish purple. Hopefully the machine was just out of color ink and not failing on her completely. Meanwhile, her computer considered the new power situation briefly, then blipped into hibernation mode, its screen going dark.

In the suddenly dim and silent room, Rebecca said, to Jeff, "I'm going to go get these pages ordered. Stay close to your fax machine."

"I knew you'd come through for me, Becca. You're the original deadline acrobat."

"Aw, shucks," she said modestly, hoping she had another color ink cartridge, and hung up before things got any worse.

Mike and Phoebe went for the "noon walk," as Phoebe called it, at 11:17. Mike could see that it was important to Phoebe to feel there was wiggle room in her daily routine now; to bust out of the in-law apartment forty-three minutes early probably felt like a jail break to her. They walked west down Judah Street toward the ocean, with Phoebe taking his arm after two blocks for support. But she was cheerful, as she almost always was these days. She told Mike that she wanted to keep going today, to go all the way to Mexico.

"We should take a left turn soon, then," Mike said. "What's in Mexico?"

"God knows," Phoebe said. "That's the *point,* dearie."

"There's a little Bethanite monastery on the Yucatán peninsula, near Guatemala. It's built near some old Mayan ruins."

"That's the kind of thing I'm talking about. Exactly."

"We'll have to be careful about drinking the water."

"You don't live to be my age without learning a thing or two about Mexican water," Phoebe said. "Is it time to rest yet?"

"Not if we're going to make it to Mexico today."

"I never said I was in a hurry," Phoebe said, and she sat on the bench at a train stop. Her favorite bench, the outer limit of her mobility now. The N-Judah drivers had long since learned not to stop for her; they would just wave as they went by. Mike sat down beside her.

"So Mary Martha is going to make her first communion?" Phoebe said when she had gotten her breath back.

Mike shrugged. "Unless I kill the pastor first. Or he kills me. She's pretty excited about it."

"I'm glad."

"We have to get her baptized first, of course."

"Oh, she's already baptized."

Mike glanced at her in surprise. "Rebecca told me—"

"What does Rebecca know?" Phoebe said. "I wanted Mary Martha baptized when she was born, but Becca wouldn't have it. So I did it myself."

Mike laughed. "Really?"

"In the bathtub. Mary Martha was about two weeks old, I think. Right after the shampoo: In the name of the Father, the Son, and the Holy Ghost, Amen."

"Lather, rinse, and repeat as necessary," Mike said.

"Do you think it counts?"

He shrugged. "*Ecce aqua: Quid prohibet me baptizari?* It's not like John the Baptist had a license. It was you or the angels, at that point."

A train rattled by, the driver waving. Phoebe waved back cheerfully.

"You can't really count on angels for anything," she noted. "As a rule."

"They mean well," Mike allowed.

"Piff," Phoebe said. It was clear what she thought of angels.

They sat quietly. The fog was burning off at last; they were beneath gray sky, but you could see blue sky and sunlight if you looked east. Like a promise.

"I think I would like a beach party for my memorial service," Phoebe said after a while.

Mike smiled. "A beach party?"

"Yes. With a band. And barbecue grills."

"No funeral mass?"

"Been there, done that." Phoebe added, "None of my old Marin County friends would be caught dead in a Catholic church anyway."

This was true enough, Mike thought. Phoebe had moved to northern California after her husband's death and had lived for several years in Stinson Beach, where she had worked part-time in an art gallery and cultivated a wide circle of friends united only by a thoroughgoing heterodoxy. Her beach parties had been legendary in their time. But it wasn't going to make it any easier to tell Rebecca her mother wanted a barbecue at her funeral.

"A beach party," he said again.

"Frisbees flying, dogs romping, the smell of hamburgers. Lovers sneaking off behind the dunes. Children making sand castles. And . . . balloons."

"Balloons!"

"Big fat ones," Phoebe said. "To be released as my ashes are given to the sea."

"You want to be cremated?"

"Yes."

"Isn't that a little, uh—"

"Un-Catholic?"

"Something like that."

Phoebe shrugged. "Ashes to ashes, sweetheart." They were silent a moment, and then she offered, as if to soften it all, "Mary Martha can supervise the balloons. And try to get Rory involved, somehow, would you? I don't want him to feel left out."

"Okay," Mike said, thinking, Thy will be done. But maybe he'd hold off for a while on telling Rebecca about the cremation. "Any particular color, on the balloons?"

"Surprise me," Phoebe said.

R ory was not at the fuse box in the garage, which was disconcerting but not surprising. Rebecca finally found him sitting at the bottom of the back steps, smoking a cigarette that turned out to be a joint. He cupped it hurriedly in his hand when he spotted her, trying to hide it, but he had a lungful of smoke, and Rebecca watched his face turn red until he finally had to release his breath in a cloud of fragrant incrimination.

"This explains a lot about the electrical situation," she said.

"No, no, I was straight when I started. This is just emergency stress relief."

Rebecca took a deep breath. She was surprised, she realized. This was, in its way, her archetypal Rory moment, caught between the crush of actuality and his blithe subversion. But what she felt was not the usual knee-jerk anger and despair, the sense of being trapped. She actually felt sad. And, even more strangely, disappointed. She had, it seemed, begun after all to tentatively believe in the miracle of Rory's turnaround.

At least, in the light of such a painful letdown, the catastrophe of the Marzipan job assumed its proper perspective as not that big a deal. But it made her wonder what it actually took to change a life, how deep you really had to go, what price you really had to pay.

Rory, also expecting her anger, seemed baffled by the lack of an explosion.

"I work better on a couple hits under stressful circumstances," he said tentatively, as if to give her a second chance to blow up. "You know that."

"You know, Rory, if it really comes down to the kitchen never being finished and you staying clean, or the kitchen being something out of *Better Homes and Gardens* with you on dope, I'll eat microwave dinners in the living room every night. It's *just not that important*. What's important is our daughter's father keeping his life together." She shook her head. "I really thought you were trying to stay clean."

"Well, *trying*," Rory said. They were silent for a moment, and then he said, a bit incredulously, "You really didn't know?"

"How the hell would I have known?"

"Phoebe didn't tell you?"

"My *mother* knew?"

Rory began to answer, then reconsidered, all too transparently. Rebecca shook her head, but she really didn't feel that she had time for the intricacies of this discussion. She said, "The reason I'm down here is not to bust you, dear. The power just went out in the whole house."

"That's probably just a fuse." Rory glanced at the still-lit joint, clearly considering taking another hit.

Rebecca said, striving for patience, "Just put it out, Rory, and get me some electricity upstairs. Jeff is holding off a bunch of suits for me downtown, and I've got to get this stuff printed."

Rory knocked the ember off the joint obligingly enough, pinched the tip and secured it with a roach clip, and slipped the joint into his pocket. "I may have to take a run to the hardware store," he said.

"Fine, but please put the fuse in first."

"No, I mean, to *buy* the fuse."

"You don't have fuses?"

"I've got twenty and thirty amps. But if the whole house blew out, we'll probably need a fifty." And, at the look on her face, "It's only a fifteen minute round-trip, Becca. I'll have you up and running in no time."

Rebecca surprised herself by laughing. There was nothing else to do but laugh.

Rory smiled uncertainly. He looked like he always looked at moments like this, like a faithful dog, a bit bewildered by all the emotional complexities but eager to do whatever he could to make it better.

"You've changed," he said.

"What?"

"You've *changed*. You've mellowed. This thing with Mike is good for you, I think."

Rebecca shook her head. She probably shouldn't have been so pleased. He was stoned, after all; the whole world looked mellower. And he had a clear self-interest in reinforcing her mildness here. But she suspected that he was actually right.

She said, "Thank you. Now, please go to the hardware store and buy the fuse you need, and a few extras to keep here in the house. Come back here and get the lights back on, or some of them, at least. And then go home to Chelsea and the baby. And count your blessings, Rory. Sober up and count your blessings, over and over again. Okay?"

"Yeah," Rory said. He got it, she saw. He really wasn't an idiot. He was just a truly wishful thinker.

The back door opened just then. It was Mike.

"Oh, hey there," he said. "I hope I'm not disturbing anything."

"We were just taking a little break," Rebecca said.

"Well, the power was out in the house. It looked like the main fuse blew, so I stuck a penny in there and it should be all right for a little while. I'm going to run up to the hardware store and get some fifty amps. Hopefully I'll be back before the place burns down. But keep an eye on it."

"Okay," Rebecca said.

Mike closed the door and was gone. Rebecca and Rory stood in silence for a moment. She could hear the chatter of her printer upstairs, as the job resumed. She had changed the ink cartridge before coming downstairs, so there was basically nothing she could do for the moment but let the world roll on. How completely weird.

She said to Rory, "Would you have thought of sticking a penny in there?"

"No way, man," Rory said. "That's dangerous. Not to mention illegal."

Chapter Eight

Jesus said to them. Daughters of Jerusalem,
do not weep for me, but for yourselves,
and for your children.

LUKE 23:28

Mike checked the address on the slip of paper, but this was definitely the place. St. Luke's Mission was housed in a decrepit old luxury hotel on Powell Street in San Francisco's Tenderloin. He slipped in through the open doors and found himself in a badly lit lobby. An enormous glass chandelier, with maybe half a dozen of its hundred tiny low-wattage bulbs burning, leaked a thin light the color of weak tea over an expanse of inert maroon carpet. To Mike's right, the elevators, with their old-fashioned iron-grate doors, were blocked off by two sawhorses with a strand of yellow crime-scene tape strung between them. Nearby, the hulk of a stuffed couch, once grand, perhaps, and perhaps once pink, had settled like a dead walrus toward something like gray. Beyond it, a set of wide stairs curved upward, the sweep of their ascent freighted with that same carpet of drearily darkening maroon, a muffling layer where light had ceased. The gray walls were punctuated by neat squares of relative white, the scars of old artwork, now filled like strange windows with graffiti, and in every corner of the place the long brown shards of long-dead ferns flopped from fat urns of greening brass.

Behind the massive oaken lobby counter, a lone woman bent over the keyboard of an ancient Macintosh computer, hacking away with singular urgency, like the telegraph operator on the *Titanic* trying to get out one last SOS before the ship went down.

"Lunch is over, dinner's not till five," she said, without looking up, as Mike approached. "We won't be registering for rooms until after dinner."

"Actually, I was here to see Father Dougherty," Mike said.

The woman paused and looked up. In the bad light it was impossible to tell her age, and it seemed likely that she didn't care in any case. She was somewhere between thirty-five and sixty years old, with unexercised laugh lines traced faintly in skin innocent of makeup, wearing a sweatshirt several sizes too large, with the sleeves rolled up, and a Forty-Niners cap. Her eyes were cool blue, and very intelligent. She looked like someone who lived with exhaustion as a matter of course, who really didn't have the time to be a human being very often, but who could rise to the occasion and even, at times, enjoy it.

"That would be Tom," she said. "He's in the kitchen, I think. Right through the dining room there, swinging doors at the back."

"Thank you," Mike said.

"You're welcome," she said. The keyboard was already click-ing again.

The hotel's banquet room, also shadowed by long-dead crys-tal chandeliers, had probably once rated three or four stars but had been converted to an efficient-looking cafeteria, with long plain tables and a lot of metal folding chairs. Each table held a funky handmade flower pot, like something from a kindergarten crafts session, and each pot had something colorful protruding from a litter of torn brown scraps of paper. The colorful bits on closer inspection turned out to be paper flowers, also of kinder-garten-level workmanship. The petals of the flowers had inspira-tional words written on them: Hope. Faith. Dignity. The brown paper scraps that served as their soil also had words on them: Bit-terness. Addiction. Despair.

Behind clean plastic cough guards, the steam tables along the food serving lines gaped empty in gleaming steel counters, by far the newest things in the place. Mike slipped through the doors at the back and found the big industrial kitchen similarly well equipped: nothing overly shiny, but everything solid and durable and well maintained. The place had the quiet air of a busy opera-tion between shifts, like a parked race car. A lone black man with a face seamed like a topographical map, wearing a hairnet and a spectacularly dirty white chef's jacket, stood by a sink full of potatoes, peeling them with a placid air.

"Father Dougherty?" Mike said.

The man laughed, revealing a profound lack of teeth and sug-gesting that you couldn't have paid him to be Father Dougherty.

"That would be Tom," he said and pointed with the peeler. "Back in the dish room."

Father Thomas Dougherty turned out to be a burly man wearing floppy rubber boots, jeans, and a black T-shirt with "St. Luke's: A Mission with a mission" stretched across his barrel chest in an ill-advised red that made the words look like a wound. He stood at the center of the dish room floor with a nozzled hose, using the stream of water to blast food scraps methodically toward a drain. The priest was built like a middle-weight fighter, with thick forearms, strenuously muscled, wiry black hair slicked to his head in sweaty eddies, and a jaw like a crag of rock, set in an igneous jut. His nose might once have been elegant, but it had been broken at least twice, and its present lines suggested pugnacity.

Dougherty glanced up as Mike entered and said, in a brusque urban Jersey accent distinct even over the noise of the water, "Lunch is over, dinner's not till five. If you're starving, Art will give you a potato."

"I'm Mike Christopher. We talked on the phone earlier."

A shard of broccoli had hung up in a crack near the sink. Dougherty directed the water and dislodged it, herding it expertly toward the drain.

"Remind me?" he said, glancing at Mike again.

"Sharon Gaston over at the NHC said you might have an opening for a hospice worker."

"Right, right." Dougherty released the nozzle trigger, and the stream of water ceased abruptly. He turned his full attention to Mike for the first time, and Mike felt the shock of his eyes, a furnace of dark brown, almost black, like a peat fire, venting an almost palpable blast of heat. In the sudden silence Mike could hear the breath whistling slightly through the mangled cartilage of the man's nose.

"So you're looking to get rich off homeless people dying, huh?" Dougherty said.

There didn't seem to be a real reply to that, and Mike said nothing. Dougherty held his gaze for a moment, then turned the hose nozzle abruptly to the wall beyond Mike's shoulder and fired a quick burst of water, blasting a cockroach that had emerged from the gap behind the sink. The bug fell to the floor, and Dougherty blew it up against the wall, played the carom expertly, and skidded the body toward the drain with the rest of the debris.

He turned to Mike again and seemed surprised to find him still there.

"Well, then—" he said resignedly, as if to say, If you insist.

Mike resisted the urge to wipe the stray water drops from his face. He had a sense of having passed some subtle but crucial aspect of the interview process, though he wasn't sure whether he was pleased about that or not. Maybe he should just have taken the potato and run. This guy was a piece of work.

"Well, then," he said.

• • •

Tuesdays, as they had been for years now, were lunch in some south-of-Market joint with Bonnie. It had started when they were both employed as artists by Utopian Images and they'd used the time after surviving Monday to reconcile themselves to the further woes of the workweek, catch up on the weekend's developments, and bitch about their jobs and love lives. Nothing much had really changed, Rebecca thought now, except that since she'd quit at Utopian Images the year before to start her own graphics business, she was up to her ears in federal small business loans, and she was paying the backbreaking self-employment tax on her own Social Security, while Bonnie still had a dental plan and got paid time and a half for overtime.

Today was Vietnamese food, and at Bonnie's insistence they both had enormous bowls of *pho.* Bonnie's latest weight-loss scheme involved eating only things that burned more calories in the labor of consuming them than they actually contained. It was a diet technically indistinguishable from starvation, and the rice noodle soup fit the agenda perfectly, especially if you used chopsticks. Bonnie was using a spoon, however, and slurping happily. She was actually somewhat perfunctory about her nutty diets since she had hooked up with Bob, who appeared perfectly content with her just the way she was.

Rebecca, who had seen herself recently in a bikini, was using chopsticks. Mike was also delighted with her just the way she was, but the old habits died hard. To complete the ritual absurdity of the whole scenario, both women had ordered big Thai beers.

The restaurant had a bit of authentic Saigon, the air thick with the smell of coriander, basil, mint, and boiling beef shin-bones. There were four angular, hoody-looking men wearing sunglasses at the back corner table, drinking iced coffee and playing cards, and the piped-in background music was mostly tinny Vietnamese covers of Wham and Madonna songs. Rebecca and Bonnie had almost gotten through the by-now-standard period of Bonnie going on and on about how great her relationship with Bob was.

While she waited for Bonnie to wind up a cute story about Bob and their dog, Rebecca reached for one of the tiny green peppers on the garnish plate and tried a bite. After the initial crunch, it didn't seem like that big a deal, but then her mouth blazed, her sinuses seized, and her eyes swelled with tears. She reached for her water, which made it worse.

"Are you okay?" Bonnie asked, briefly distracted from her own half-full glass.

Rebecca nodded, trying to breathe without moving any more air through her inflamed passages.

"Pepper," she managed at last.

Bonnie looked relieved. Rebecca's emotional life was often a mystery to her. "They're very hot."

Rebecca flagged their waiter and pointed desperately to her beer bottle, an SOS, and the guy nodded and hustled off. She drained the dregs of the first Singha, which also didn't help, blew her nose into her napkin, and, steering with the skid, took the opportunity to say to Bonnie, "Mary Martha has started going to morning mass with Mike."

Her friend looked appropriately astounded. "How in the world does he get her out of bed?"

"She sets her own alarm."

"Wow." Bonnie hesitated, in obvious caution. Rebecca knew her friend was on the verge of telling some edifying story about Bob and their own Episcopalian church. Bob's church, Rebecca knew. Bonnie just went for the pleasure of sitting beside her husband in the pew, because happy married people went to church together. It was a dress-up opportunity, essentially, and they went out for pancakes afterward. Bonnie had been raised in some relatively harmless Protestant sect and was undamaged by dogma and fanaticism. And Bob's God was a genial midlevel managerial type. It was just one more thing that had become difficult for Rebecca to talk with her friend about.

She said quickly, to head off any digressions, "The parish priest wants her to make her first communion, and Mary Martha is all for it. The guy even asked Mike to teach the class."

"I'll bet Mike's great with kids," Bonnie said supportively, missing the point.

"Mary Martha hasn't even been baptized," Rebecca said.

"Ah."

"I never wanted her to have to deal with all that stuff."

"Rebecca, you married a *monk*. You shouldn't be surprised to find out he's Catholic. And besides, what can it hurt?"

"Bonnie, these people are maniacs. It's like the Chinese with little girls' feet. My soul has a permanent limp."

"Mike's not a maniac."

This was, Rebecca knew, a high compliment from Bonnie, who cherished innocuousness. "Well, not an orthodox one," she said. "I mean, at least he's not opposed to birth control."

Bonnie was silent at that, and Rebecca realized at once that she had blundered. Bonnie and Bob were intent on having a baby, so far without luck. She said, "Oops. Sorry, sweetie."

"It's okay," Bonnie said. "We're going to go see someone, actually. A specialist."

"Really?"

"Bob's afraid it's him."

"Ouch."

"I'm afraid it's *me*."

"Maybe it's not anybody. Maybe it's just, uh—" Destiny, Rebecca thought, and held her tongue. Or, worse, because more meaningless, luck. Or God, worst of all, because completely inscrutable. The big out-of-your-hands elements. She really had nothing of comfort to offer here.

"Whatever it is, I'm not getting any younger," Bonnie said. "But the technology has gotten very sophisticated."

She seemed satisfied enough with that. Bonnie had real faith in managed processes. Bob had three shelves of books on Relationship, and the Schofields steered by them religiously. No doubt they were already accumulating books on procreation.

"You and Bob will be wonderful parents," Rebecca said.

"How about you guys?" Bonnie said. "Any luck there?"

Rebecca shook her head vaguely. Bonnie, she knew, would be horrified by the truth: Rebecca and Mike hadn't even discussed the question of children. It just, weirdly, hadn't come up yet. She suspected that it might be a given that they would not have kids, Mike was such a different kind of animal in so many ways. It was as if she had married outside her species. Anything they produced would be a radical hybrid and probably as sterile as a mule.

In any case, the whole issue was way too complicated to discuss with Bonnie anymore. Bonnie would just feel sorry for her. Rebecca had married a guy who might be a saint in the making and who certainly had saintlike qualities—absolutely incomprehensible reserves of patience, tenderness, and unselfishness—but who also, in the world's usual terms and values, was more or less useless. If what Mike had could be bottled and sold, they would be rich, but in practice she and Mary Martha and Phoebe seemed to get it all. It didn't translate well, it didn't show up on a résumé, and it certainly didn't pay. It was beautiful and delicate and absolutely unremunerative, and Rebecca sometimes wondered if she really had the guts for this, playing chicken with such fundamental insecurity, her deepest, truest self with the pedal to the metal of love and beauty, heading straight toward the most obvious and seemingly inevitable crash.

Oh, well, she thought. There were certain benefits to going down the tubes for beauty and God, to being poor and in love. A year ago, after all, she had just been poor.

Rebecca's second beer arrived, and she took a tentative sip. It still felt like raw coals inside her mouth. She said, frankly striking out for fresh territory, "I may have to hire somebody for the business."

"That's great!" Bonnie said. "I mean, isn't it?"

"It will be if I can afford it. I'm afraid I've got just enough work right now for one person to be overloaded. Thank God Phoebe is paying rent on the in-law apartment."

"How's Mike's job hunt going?"

"He just sort of seems to be ambling along waiting for God to hook him up. Though he did finally take that hospice training course, so he's got a piece of paper. But that was money going out, not money coming in."

"How much?" Bonnie asked, ever practical.

"I don't know. He put it on his credit card." They smiled at that. Mike's credit card, his first piece of plastic in twenty years rattling around in his naked wallet, was an ongoing amusement to them. The credit industry had no idea. Rebecca said, "I actually find myself sometimes wishing he'd go back to McDonald's. Just to get some money coming in. Isn't that horrible? The glory days when his career as a hamburger cook was on track."

"We ate there several times," Bonnie said. "He was good."

"They were going to move him up to the counter, but he didn't want to shave that often."

"We still have to have you guys over soon."

Rebecca nodded. They'd already let several weekends slip by without fulfilling their dinner date with the Schofields. Rebecca had pleaded reentry overload, child care issues, work stuff, and even actual illness once, but the fact was, it was almost impossible to imagine sitting in a room with just her, Mike, Bonnie, and Bob. Mike was vaguely willing to go through with the exercise, in principle, but in practice he seemed much happier every time Rebecca managed to put it off and they could just slip a video into the machine and get in bed early.

Bonnie, who probably understood most of this herself, said, with a sly trace of blame-it-on-the-boys camaraderie, "Tell Mike he doesn't have to shave."

Rebecca laughed. It was a glimpse of the Bonnie she loved best, the true friend utterly in tune with the realities and trickiness of human relationships and willing to work with her on it. She offered, in essential confirmation of Bonnie's guess, "I think it will be easier, somehow, once he's got a job and his male ego can calm down a little. I mean, he's *Mike,* you know, he looks like he's contemplating the Trinity most of the time and is surprised every time he has to put a quarter in a parking meter, but I know it pains him to not be bringing money in."

"Mike will get work," Bonnie said stoutly. "And your business is taking off. You'll hire somebody, and grow, and hire somebody else, and the next thing you know you'll be a capitalist pig vacationing in the Bahamas."

"I suppose. I'm going to have to rent office space at some point. It's sort of hard to picture an employee working with me in the dining room." She gave Bonnie a glance. "I don't suppose you want a job?"

Bonnie's face froze for an instant, and in her friend's dismay Rebecca caught a glimpse of the thinness of the limb she was actually out on.

"Just kidding," she said quickly.

"It's just—well, you know, with wanting the baby and all, we really need my health plan right now. And Jeff has promised to spring for paid maternity leave, when the time comes."

"Of course, of course. I really was just yanking your chain."

Their waiter appeared just then, to their mutual relief. "You ladies like coffee?"

Bonnie glanced at her watch. "Oh, man, I really should get back."

"Just the check," Rebecca told the guy, and, to Bonnie, as he nodded and moved off, "on me, today."

"Nonsense."

"Nonsense yourself. I'm an embryonic capitalist pig, I'm halfway to the damn Bahamas."

Bonnie visibly weighed it out. They usually just threw mutually approximate amounts of cash on the table and called it even, but they both knew that Bonnie had shown her cards already today by being appalled at Rebecca's failures of practicality, and that to insist now would only make it worse, and Bonnie finally conceded, "My turn next time."

"Unless Mike's with us," Rebecca said. "Then we'll just put it on his credit card."

Bonnie laughed, which was really the best they were going to be able to do at this point, dignity-wise. Rebecca laid down the last bills in her wallet, overtipping blatantly, and they hurried out before further damage could be done.

Everything in the garden was dead again except the poppies and the squash. The poppies were spectacular and self-propagating, pure grace, and the squash was simply stolid and more or less indestructible in a squash kind of way, sprouted from old seeds in the compost. In neither case was there really much for Phoebe to do except maybe a bit of weeding. The garden was only about as big as a good throw quilt anyway. If she'd had a bigger bit of land to work with and been somewhere with enough sun to grow tomatoes, it might have been a different story. But this little bit of her daughter's foggy backyard wasn't enough to keep her on the planet. Still, it was good exercise as far as it went. Phoebe felt that on the whole she was getting stronger and that soon, quite soon, with the grace of God, she might be strong enough to die.

It seemed to come down to whether to trust her sense of what was real or not. Because what seemed real now had diverged from what everyone else was paying attention to most of the time. Phoebe felt like she'd been in a play—not a bad play, either, a wonderful play—and that the good long run of the production was over and it was time to strike the set and see what was next, but the other actors didn't seem to realize it. They just went on and on, playing the same roles in the empty theater. She would have liked to have helped them catch up, but there were more important things to be attended to.

And so Phoebe walked west. In the early days after the stroke it had been all she could do to get herself upright and make it to the bathroom, and then for a long time, months, she had been confined to the house, and then the backyard, which had seemed enormous then. Eventually she had gotten to the point of being able to take short walks outside—to the corner and back at first, and then gradually farther along Judah Street, working her way block by block through the avenues toward the sea. It was ten blocks from the corner of Rebecca's street to the end of the N-Judah train line at 48th, and downhill all the way; beyond that was a line of dunes, the Great Highway, and a final set of dunes before the Pacific itself. Phoebe could get as far as the 7-Eleven at 45th Avenue now before her body crapped out on her and dissolved into trembling and she had to take the train home, feeling her muscles like melted butter and her heart in her chest like a jackhammer.

The way she saw it now, it didn't matter much: If she died on the sidewalk, dying en route to death, as it were, great. If she died on the train home, awkward but not really so terrible. And if she made it to the sea, best of all. In any case, she was doing what she had to do, what God had given her now, and walking toward death. It wasn't like there were style points awarded; it wasn't figure skating, for God's sake. All you really had to do, once you'd picked up the cross, was try to keep moving.

Tom Dougherty's office looked about like what you would expect from a guy who dealt with cockroaches with a hose, who also had paperwork. The room was tiny, and the single window looked out onto the brick wall of an alley. Mike had to move a large pile of folders containing grant applications from the room's lone visitor's chair while Dougherty settled behind the desk, which had three tall sprawling piles of paper. In, out, and miscellaneous, maybe. He was still wearing the floppy rubber boots. Mike had a sense of being a temporary inconvenience between bouts in the dish room.

Dougherty glanced at Mike's résumé and grunted. "Big gap here. Jail time?"

"Monastery."

"No shit?"

"No shit."

"Out of the frying pan, into the fire," Dougherty said. He leaned back in his chair and put his feet up on the corner of the desk. There was a well-maintained clear space there, the only one available, obviously for that purpose. "Why'd you quit?"

"I was pissed off at my abbot."

"That's a lousy reason."

Mike shrugged. He didn't have a good reason. He still wasn't sure there was one.

Dougherty eyed him for a moment, then said, "Just so we're clear: I have neither the time nor the patience to waste five minutes, much less twenty years, on you being pissed off at me."

"I'll try to be efficient about it, then."

The corner of Dougherty's mouth turned up slightly. He swung his feet down off the desk and tossed Mike's résumé toward one of the piles of paper, where it settled into instant obscurity, like sand on a beach.

"Well, here's the deal," he said. "Our usual work here is just serving as a hard place for people to hit bottom. We try to feed and shelter them until they stop bouncing and see what's next. But we just got a big chunk of money specifically to fund a hospice program." Dougherty shook his head. "A million bucks for dying homeless people. Can you believe that shit?"

Mike shrugged. Hard to believe that shit, indeed.

"If they'd give us a million bucks for food, addiction programs, and job training, we could keep a lot more of them from dying, of course, but some rich guy stubbed his toe on a corpse one night on Turk Street after the theater let out and so we've got money to burn for a while on morphine drips and beds that crank into different positions and RNs to tell us when the guys have stopped breathing." Dougherty stood up abruptly. "Do you smoke?"

"Yes," Mike said, wondering if that was in the job description.

Dougherty crossed to the door. "Felicity, if the mayor calls, I'm in conference," he called to the woman behind the lobby counter, who was still hammering away at her keyboard.

"Yeah, right," Felicity said without looking up, obviously on to him.

Dougherty closed the door and went to the window, lifted the sash, and sat down on the sill. There was an implicit invitation in it all, and Mike joined him, sitting on the other side of the wide sill. Dougherty produced a pack of Marlboro Reds and offered Mike one, then lit both their cigarettes on a single match. He took the long first drag of an addict toward the end of his comfort zone and leaned slightly out into the alley to blow the smoke away.

"Try to keep it outside," he told Mike. "Felicity gets really pissed off if she can smell it."

Mike blew his own smoke carefully toward the brick wall. The air from the alley was fog-chilly and smelled of rotten bananas and urine.

"So, where were we?" Dougherty said.

"A million bucks for dying homeless people. The irony."

"The thing is, I haven't got a minute for it. I'm trying to keep the bastards alive on pennies. So I need somebody who can handle the shit day-to-day, somebody I can blame for the cluster fucks at funding reviews, and somebody who can at least give the occasional appearance of these guys checking out with dignity and oh by the way make damn sure there aren't any more bodies on Geary Street. You wouldn't think it's rocket science, but I've run through three people on it in the last month and a half."

"I can't imagine why," Mike said.

"It's a mystery," Dougherty agreed cheerfully. "Did you happen to notice our table decorations in the cafeteria?"

"The vases and paper flowers?"

"That was our last hospice gal's arts-and-crafts program for the dying. She was a pretty little thing with a bachelor's in social work and a master's in Kübler-Ross or something. Cute as a button. She had all the guys making Dignity Flowers affirming their inherent value as human beings. But she couldn't stop the bastards from selling their morphine and using the money to buy Night Train."

Dougherty's cigarette ember was already at the filter; he smoked harder than anyone Mike had ever seen. The priest looked at the butt as if it had let him down, then flicked it out into the alley. Mike, his cigarette only halfway through, hesitated before following suit.

"It's an alley, for Christ's sake," Dougherty said. "Just don't drop it on the body there." And, as Mike involuntarily glanced down, "Hah, made you look."

Mike disposed of his butt, and Dougherty shut the window and went back to his desk. Mike started back to his own chair, but the priest said, "Okay, then, room 215."

"What's in room 215?"

"I thought you said you wanted a job," Dougherty said.

•　•　•

When Rebecca got back to her car, she found that it had been ticketed. She had parked at a metered spot on Third Street near Howard, half a block from the Museum of Modern Art, and had loaded the meter with every coin she had before lunch, but apparently she had missed the deadline by a matter of minutes. She could still see the back of the traffic cop's little golf cart, working its way up the block toward Mission. It was maddening, and beyond ironic: throw in the face-saving gesture at lunch, and this little jaunt had already cost her more money than she could possibly make this afternoon even if she hurried home right now and got right to work like the diligent neo-Puritan entrepreneur she was supposed to be.

Instead, she left the ticket on the windshield and walked up the street to the MOMA. There was a Franz Marc show in town that she'd been meaning to get to for weeks. If the day was going to be a total disaster, at least she could do something for her real self. She already had her purse open at the admissions window when she realized that she'd left the last bills in her wallet on the table at the restaurant.

It was, cumulatively, enough to make even a firm believer question God's sense of humor, if not His actual existence. Rebecca stood on the sidewalk for a long moment, wishing that she was already home and could just cut her losses on the day and pour a glass of wine and curl up on the couch with Mike. He would laugh when she ran out her new theory of petty urban indignities as the real cause of the loss of faith circa the second millenium.

"Excuse me, are you in line?" a woman behind her asked. A tourist, a kind-faced, matronly woman with an air of Midwestern sobriety, wearing an Alcatraz sweatshirt colored penal gray, like homelessness, but brand-new. Her husband had the exact same sweatshirt but seemed less happy about it.

"Not unless you want to loan me $12.50," Rebecca said.

The woman looked briefly alarmed, then realized that Rebecca was kidding, probably. "I thought you didn't need any money to get in today," she said.

"What?"

The woman pointed to the sign. At the bottom of all the other, somewhat intricate fees for every age and category of person, a grace line read "First Tuesday of Every Month: Admission Free."

"I think I just had a religious experience," Rebecca said to the woman.

"So you *are* in line, then?"

"I suppose I am," Rebecca said, wondering why, in the light of such divine beneficence, she still felt slightly grudging. But she realized that some niggling part of her brain was still doing the math. A $40 parking ticket versus the $12.50 admission fee: if there really was a God at work here, she couldn't help but think He still owed her $27.50.

•   •   •

She was ashamed of her pettiness as soon as she was in the gallery. Franz Marc had changed her life when she was fourteen years old. She had been a horse girl, had been drawing and painting horses since she had first picked up a crayon, and had long since worked her way through Remington and Russell, Reginald Jones and George Stubbs, to the stylized Appaloosas of Carol Grigg, but she was feeling a vague cosmic discontent by then. Her ninth-grade boyfriend, Peter, had kissed her for the first time the week before, and it had torn a ragged place in her world. Peter was reading Schopenhauer, which Rebecca knew now was probably a very bad sign in a teenager, but at the time his gloominess had had an extraordinary appeal. She had tried to read Schopenhauer too, but by then Peter was in volume two of *The World as Will and Representation* and she had had the feeling she would never catch up even if she was able to read Kant, which he seemed to think was a prerequisite. But the relationship had destabilized her sense of beauty and made her regret her own simplicities. She was afraid Peter would not kiss her again if she did not have some insight. And so she had taken the train into Manhattan with her friend Margaret and gone to the Museum of Modern Art. It was Peter's view that only music, and possibly only Mahler, truly qualified as art, but he was also reading Kandinsky on the spiritual and was prepared to concede some value to paintings as long as they did not slavishly depict actual things.

The relationship had not lasted very long. Peter was not a good enough kisser, it turned out, for Rebecca to ever really warm up to pure abstraction, and her next boyfriend, Steve, had been a very good kisser and had not cared what she painted, as long as she let him get to second base, which was also her sense of where Mike stood. But she had loved Marc from the moment she saw her first blue horse, and it had set something inside her free.

Two steps into the SFMOMA gallery now, standing in front of *Die grossen blauen Pferde,* three plump horses of softened cobalt curled into themselves in a brick red landscape that echoed the sumptuous lines of their backs, Rebecca felt the hush of pure seeing coming upon her. She had a weird but distinct sense that she had not moved a step since that day in New York. It was the same painting and she was the same person. She had learned nothing, had accomplished nothing; she had disappeared somehow; she might as well have fallen asleep and just awakened. She realized that she was afraid: seeing this way was something like truth for her, an aspect of her real self, forgotten for ages and suddenly present, and to feel this was to feel how long it had been since she felt this way, to face the reality of her prolonged distraction. If she was honest with herself, in this light, she could not help but feel she had wasted the past quarter century. This glimpse, this vision, was a promise to herself that she had utterly failed to keep.

But the condition was strangely forgiving; the waste of the last twenty-five years actually seemed like small change given to a beggar in the immediacy of this seeing. And what could she have done differently, in any case? It wasn't as if she should have stayed with Peter, who had in his way driven her to that first moment.

Peter had just gotten gloomier and more eccentric, had gone on to Nietzsche and then Heidegger and then some sort of Eastern thing that involved shaving his head; there had been a couple halfhearted suicide attempts, and he had finally gone back to school and majored in history, and the last she had heard of him he had married someone blond and was thriving in all the obvious ways as a corporate lawyer.

No, all she could imagine having done for the last decades to avoid the humiliating lapse of reality was standing in front of this painting, letting the crowds come and go around her day by day, sidestepping the mops of the janitors at night. The texture of the paint on the canvas, a bit pebbly here and there, or smoothed and fading at the end of a stroke, seemed like the only thing vivid enough to have held onto. She could feel that this painting was unfinished and her own brush was laden with that blue, and that she had simply paused to consider the next stroke. And what was twenty-five years, in that light? She still didn't know the next stroke, there was only this seeing that was a kind of waiting, like a fire that had smoked through all those years over dirty fuel and flirted with dying, and was settling at last into clear bright burning. If it had taken twenty-five years to burn this cleanly, so be it; she was just happy that it had. The years between seeing like this didn't matter, and all her failures and falseness did not matter. What mattered was only what had always mattered, what she had lost sight of in the fog of living and now saw clearly through the grace of a perverse God and parking tickets and free Tuesdays at

SFMOMA; and all that mattered now was all that had ever mattered, to just find a way to keep on seeing it.

T he man in room 215 was dead. He lay on the elevated hospital bed, staring up at the ceiling, smoke damaged from some long-ago fire, with unseeing blue eyes like two cold marbles. One corner of his mouth had turned up into an unsoothable snarl, already frozen, unnervingly, into place. Mike wondered briefly whether this was some kind of perverse initiation ordeal concocted by Dougherty, then realized, no, the priest really hadn't known. The man had just died, during lunch.

Beyond the room's window, the same brick wall stoppered the view like a cork. So casual was this death, so banal, lonely, and unnoticed, that the man might almost have simply crawled behind the trash cans in the alley one floor below. Except then he wouldn't have had morphine to steal. The snapped plastic line still ran uselessly from the man's arm toward the empty IV rack by the bed. Mike hoped whoever had taken the drug had had the grace to wait until the guy was dead.

He sat down in the chair beside the bed. The swing-away bedside table was littered with sheets of purple, pink, and red construction paper, some safety scissors, a few magic markers, and a small heap of brown paper scraps inscribed with things like *drugs* and *poor mony managment.*

Mike swung the table out of the way for the moment, opened his battered monastery breviary, and began the office of the dead. *Libera me, Domine, de morte æterna.* There would be time later, he thought, there really was nothing but time, to finish the poor guy's Dignity Flower.

Chapter Nine

My grace is sufficient for thee; your strength is made perfect in weakness.

2 CORINTHIANS 12:9

Saturday mornings were Mary Martha's soccer games. Mary Martha had been playing since she was four, and in previous years Rebecca had just come to the games alone and done minimal bonding with the other mothers, shivering in the foggy meadows of Golden Gate Park and watching the adorable huddle of small children with the ball at the center move vaguely around the field like a drunken swarm of bees. But this year Rory in his new incarnation as gung-ho quasi-suburban dad was coaching the team, and the games had somehow become communal events requiring furniture, coolers, blankets, a staggering amount of equipment to carry from the distant parking spots. In addition to Mike and Phoebe, Rory's girlfriend, Chelsea, attended. She and Rory had married the previous March, just in time for the birth of their child, but it was still hard for Rebecca to think of her as his wife. She was wearing a gorgeous Guatemalan serape that smelled distinctly of hemp, which she would lift occasionally to breast-feed the baby, whose name was Stuart John, after both Rory's and Chelsea's fathers, and who was called Stu-J. Rebecca, who knew Rory's father, Stuart, a rigid alcoholic welder embittered by the demise of the steel industry in Pittsburgh, had been blindsided by poignancy at the name; she and Rory too had planned to name their first son after both grandfathers, and her father's name too had been John. Stu-J was a magnificently serene child with Chelsea's lopsided vulnerable mouth and strawberry-blond hair and Rory's alert blue eyes, which meant that he had Mary Martha's eyes, which was emotionally confusing.

They set up their line of folding lawn chairs along the vaguely marked sideline of the field while the Sunset Sharks took warm-up shots at one end and some team from the Richmond district warmed up at the other. Phoebe sat to Rebecca's right, wrapped in an enormous quilt and ostensibly doing needlepoint. But the pillow she had been working on for the last three months, a seascape, had shown no perceptible progress for weeks now; it was Rebecca's impression, indeed, that Phoebe's sessions now were tilted slightly toward a net unraveling effect. But her mother seemed perfectly content with that, and she settled in quickly to her semblance of industry. Chelsea sat to Rebecca's left, with Stu-J sleeping for the moment in a portable bassinet beside her. Mike was over with the team; he had drifted into a de facto assistant coaching role on game days, and

Rory had actually been trying for a while now to get him to come to the practices too.

A soccer coach and a Sunday school teacher, Rebecca thought, looking at her once and present husbands now. She'd come a long way from sleeping in the back of a VW van in Santa Cruz, selling watercolors on the boardwalk to buy paint, Cheez Whiz, and dope while Rory surfed.

"Mike is so nice," Chelsea said, following Rebecca's eyes.

Rebecca nodded. Mike, she knew, was really not all that nice, in a socially virtuous sense, and could in fact be obstinate, disruptive, and even fierce when pressed too far. What he was, was almost unfailingly kind, which in practice usually amounted to the same thing.

She said, "Rory's mellowed quite a bit over the years too," and wondered immediately whether that sounded condescending or even snarky, but Chelsea just nodded happily. She was a relative innocent with a very straightforward good heart and a half-full-glass view of human nature, which had clearly been what Rory needed; anyone who'd had his number from the start or been inclined to look too closely or really seen him in anything but the sweetest mild light of love would have been out of there long since. He had his strengths, but waiting for them to manifest had always required a near-saintly patience.

Out on the field, Rory blew his whistle to call the team together for the final huddle before the start of the game. Rory, with a whistle. It was at least as strange as the pocket calendar. He was wearing a clean sweatshirt advertising the team's sponsor, Starbucks, and a ball cap with a shark logo on it, the bill pointed toward the front. Rebecca had never before seen him wear a hat that was not turned backward.

"I think he's been more stressed out lately," Chelsea said.

Probably withdrawal symptoms, Rebecca thought, but she managed to hold her tongue. She was still feeling her way into how to converse with Chelsea without leaking bitterness, cynicism, or any of her own cumulative disillusionment. And not just with Rory: talking with Chelsea often made Rebecca feel ancient, world-weary, and mean in general. She said, "Well, he's got a lot on his plate right now. He's taken on a lot of responsibilities. It's new territory for him, no offense, in a lot of ways."

"I think he needs to surf more," Chelsea said, and Rebecca laughed in spite of herself. "No, seriously. It's been weeks, I think, since he got to the beach at all."

"No, no, I know you're serious," Rebecca said. "You may even be right. It's just—well, you know, forgive me, but getting to the beach has just never really been a problem for Rory in the past."

"I understand," Chelsea said. "Rory has told me a lot about your relationship. He feels bad now about so many things."

It was a tiny shock to realize that, of course, Rory had discussed and even, almost unimaginably, analyzed his relationship history with Chelsea. Rebecca found herself stumped for a reply, and even for a tone for a reply, but fortunately, the game was beginning.

Mary Martha ran by them on the way to her position and bypassed the grown-ups to drop down in front of Stu-J and coo at him fondly for a moment. Rebecca watched her, feeling a distinct tug at her heart; it was a moment to sharply feel something that had been emerging slowly but surely all along, that Mary Martha had a brother. Rebecca felt unnervingly out of that relationship loop; she had tried, in her few opportunities, to find an emotional approach to Stu-J, something warm if not actually auntlike, but so far she had failed to connect. Seeing the depth of Mary Martha's love now was a bit of a jolt.

A whistle blew on the field and Mary Martha scrambled to her feet, blew them a kiss, and ran out to her position. She looked strangely sturdy in her baggy shorts, with the shin guards beneath her kneesocks; and the teal jersey brought out an unexpected tinge of green in her eyes. Growing up, Rebecca realized. Becoming a kid among kids.

"You go, girl!" she hollered, and her daughter smiled shyly and gave her a thumbs-up, then assumed a self-conscious position of readiness, her hands on her knees. The ball was kicked into play and the game began. It was a bit more coherent this year, with some of the kids occasionally dribbling for a few steps or even trying to pass, but for the most part it was still the same mad scramble.

Stu-J, roused by the sudden flurry, began to stir and whimper, and Chelsea bent to attend to him. Phoebe had gone off to the bathroom, a walk of about a hundred yards, well within her range these days; and Rebecca took advantage of the brief interval of relative privacy to take out her cell phone and dial Mike's number. He had his phone turned on all the time now, she knew, in case one of his dying people called with a crisis. Rebecca was still amazed at how happy Mike seemed to be with his new job. He liked his boss, a cantankerous old renegade priest who smoked and swore and drank like a fish; and he even seemed to like the people he was working with, mostly down-and-out guys with their livers failing and their lungs shot, malnourished, demoralized, often strangely fatalistic about their last decline. He'd already had three people die on his watch, not counting the first guy, who had already been dead. How he came home after work like that and played with Mary Martha and drank a beer and watched the sunset with Rebecca was beyond her comprehension, but it was a tremendous relief to their budget at this point. Mike had actually forgotten to ask what his salary was in his initial interview, and they'd had to wait for his first paycheck to find out what he was making. It had turned out to be slightly more than he'd made cooking hamburgers and somewhat less than he could have made as a decent janitor. Not a lot, not even necessarily enough, but way better than nothing. Rebecca had made him ask about the health plan, and Dougherty had laughed and told Mike that the health plan at St. Luke's was to get sick and die.

From her seat, Rebecca could see Mike on the sideline among the Sharks' substitute players, towering over them; when his phone rang, he reached for it with a jerk, as if he had been stung by a bee. She could hear the caution in his voice as he answered. "Hello?"

"Hey, baby," she said. "Have I got a job for *you*."

"Thank God," Mike said. "I thought someone was going to make me do actual work."

"We'll have to discuss remuneration, of course."

"Oh, I'll remunerate you."

"No, I mean your salary, sweetie."

"Well, I'd certainly expect to make at least as much as I made in my last position."

"Would that be your time as a line production manager at McDonalds, Inc.?"

"No, I was referring to my twenty years with the Bethanite corporation."

"Ah, yes, I have your résumé here. So you're saying you'd like to make at least—let me crunch the numbers for a moment—nothing?"

"I think I've demonstrated that I'm worth it."

"You're hired. When can you start?"

"Well, did you bring a blanket? I'm thinking that eucalyptus grove over there."

"Mr. Christopher, I'm shocked—shocked!—that you would even consider neglecting your coaching duties. But right after the game would be good."

Mike barked. It took her off guard, as it always did. It was the most amazing little sexual yip, richly suggestive somehow, even slightly obscene. Rebecca giggled and glanced self-consciously over at the Sharks' sideline, but no one there seemed unduly perturbed by their assistant coach's barking.

"You really should not be allowed out in public, sir," she said, and clicked off before he could bark again. Beside her, Chelsea had picked up Stu-J and was bouncing him gently on her lap and attending to the game with such explicit absorption that Rebecca realized that the younger woman had probably gotten most of the flavor of the exchange. She considered trying to salvage some semblance of dignity, then decided it was too late for that and went for girl talk instead.

"That man," she said. "He *barked* at me."

Chelsea smiled appreciatively. "Rory growls."

"I know."

"Oh, yeah, right." Their eyes met, and they smiled; it was an unprecedented moment. God help us, Rebecca thought. We may end up being friends.

Stu-J, perhaps feeling neglected, said, "*Ga!*" and both women took the opportunity to quit while they were ahead and attend to him. Rebecca held out her hand toward him, and the baby grabbed one of her fingers and examined it

"He is *so* adorable," Rebecca said. "Such a sweet-natured kid."

"Thank you."

"Do you mind if I hold him?"

"That would be cool," Chelsea said, and swung Stu-J over into Rebecca's arms. "Say hi to your Auntie Beck, Stu-J."

All the old instincts were back in play instantly. Stu-J molded himself into the curve of her arm as if he'd been born for it and considered her with those blue, blue eyes, with all their echoes and immediacy. He smelled of talc and strawberries and that indefinable tang of sheer babyness. Rebecca felt her heart hurt, her womb ache, her eyes fill. It was a little unnerving.

"Boogadoogascooga," she said, and Stu-J grinned his off-kilter grin, pleased and amused, and said, "Ga."

I t was possible to move from silence to silence, Phoebe had discovered. A new way of traveling, like crossing a desert, from oasis to oasis. There was the din and the blare and the pain, comfortless and grueling, like sand and sun glare on dry rock, and the hot wind of empty activity everywhere. And love dried up and hope dried up and there was only faith, sun-blinded, mute, and desiccate in a world that had dried up into its own noise. Your body became a stranger, something yoked to you, like a dying camel, and the sweetness of memory dribbled away like water into sand. Every effort only seemed to take you deeper into that waste, and every direction was that waste, forever. And yet there was nothing to do but go on. The old maps meant nothing. You simply went on into the mystery of that harsh, parched vastness, from agony to dry agony.

But there were spots, as sudden as dreams, but realer than that, as water was realer than dryness. Like the world at dawn, remembering color, like a jackhammer stopping. And in that peace you knew that the desert was a nightmare only and it had been love all along. It had only taken this dying to know it. And even when you found, incomprehensibly, that there were somehow more steps to

be taken, it was easier somehow, lighter, knowing that you only had
to get this dying right.

I t wasn't until halftime that they realized Phoebe was gone,
and even then it took a while to sink in. It had been
Rebecca's impression that her mother could only walk a
couple hundred yards anyway, but Mike, who had been paying
closer attention, said that she was up to over a half mile lately.

They checked the women's bathroom, and then the men's,
and circled the entire meadow once, and by then it was time for
the second half to start and therefore time to decide whether to
truly panic and call an immediate and complete halt to normality
or not. Rebecca was inclined to start screaming and have every
one of the half dozen soccer games in progress on the meadow
cease at once, to get everyone looking for her mother, but Mike
said he thought Phoebe might have just gone over to the tulip
garden or something, and in any case he thought he could find
her by the end of the game, at which point, if Phoebe was still
AWOL, Rebecca could sound as loud an alarm as she liked.

It did make sense, Rebecca had to concede, to not freak
Mary Martha out unless it was absolutely necessary, not to mention the rest of the team and the rest of the league. But the sobriety of being a mother was the only thing between her and a
daughter's visceral panic, and the line was feeling very thin. She
hadn't felt this helpless and terrified since Phoebe's first stroke,

when her mother had collapsed at Rebecca's feet on a Mission Street sidewalk after lunch the previous October.

"Call me as soon as you find her," she told Mike.

"Of course."

"I mean, the *second* you find her. If you see her in the distance, call me then. Call me if you find a footprint, call me if you have a strong *intuition* of finding her."

"I have a strong intuition of finding her," Mike said. "Now go cheer for Mary Martha, before she starts thinking something's up."

T he roar before her was the sea at last; and behind her was the roar of the world. They blended at moments, like whirlwinds colliding, and her blood was roaring in her ears. Her bones hurt so, a useless skeleton sinking through her weakness, as her feet sank into the sand without progressing. Nothing firm left but her aching bones and the muscles would not carry. There was no sorting it out now, the time for worrying over thoughts was past, but the roar of her thoughts was pain now too, and there was no explaining, could be no explaining. That might have been the worst pain, that love could not explain to love love's ways. The sea might wash even that away, but distance had become strange and it was possible the sea was the future and the roar behind her was the past and the roar within her was the dying that went on all the time. The cries of the damned were everywhere, and she listened for her own voice among them. But words were gone, and the sand should not have been so cold and it was possible she was dead, though if she was dead it seemed that the roar and the pain should have ceased should have ceased and the confusion so maybe but.

And then Mike was there, which in its way was more confusing still.

"How did you find me?" Phoebe said.

"You only go west," Mike said, tucking the blanket he had brought under her chin. "If you ever change that, we're all screwed."

"I'm waiting for John."

"I hope he has a boat."

"Oh, yes."

"Good," Mike said. "Can I help you up?"

"I think I'd like to sit for a while, if you don't mind."

"Not at all," Mike said, and he sat down beside her on the sand.

"Is there trouble?" Phoebe said. And, as Mike looked uncertain, "Among the living, I mean?"

"Not if we get back by the end of the game."

"The game is over, dearie."

"Not for Mary Martha."

"Ahh," Phoebe said, impressed. She used to be able to keep track of that stuff too. "Of course. A time to live, and a time to die, right?"

"Right," Mike said. "But I don't think it's your time to die today, Phoebe. No offense."

"None taken," Phoebe said. "It appears that you are right."

They sat quietly for a while, watching the gulls whirl and screech. A line of pelicans went past, earnest and orderly. It wasn't heaven, but it wasn't bad.

After a while Mike said, almost apologetically, "I should call Rebecca."

"Rebecca's still alive?"

"Yes."

"And John? Is he still alive?"

"No," Mike said.

"Ah, that's where you're wrong," Phoebe said. "John has a boat."

B ack at the house, they ordered the traditional postgame pizzas and broke out the traditional postgame beer for the adults and juices for the kids, as if everything were normal. Mary Martha had brought a friend home, a teammate named Zoe, and Zoe's parents were there, very nice people. The girls ran upstairs to play with Mary Martha's American Girl dolls, and the adults sat down in the living room with the refrigerator and the stove, and everyone cooed over Stu-J and made soccer parent talk. It was a near-perfect performance of the usual Saturday scene, Rebecca thought, and thank God for that. When you had kids, basically, the show had to go on, pretty much no matter what.

Mike, meanwhile, took Phoebe straight downstairs, put her to bed, and made her soup. Rebecca let him handle it by himself, feeling guilty about that. Her mother was gray with cold and fatigue, and shivering uncontrollably; she looked heartbreakingly frail, as bad as she had looked for months. Rebecca thought that she probably could have handled that, but Phoebe kept making cryptic little remarks that indicated she was completely whacked out as well, and the specter of her mother's growing dementia was just too much. If it hadn't been for Mike, Rebecca knew, she would have taken Phoebe straight to the hospital and let strangers deal with her.

She hated herself for that; she felt it as a shameful emotional failure. In the hospital the previous fall, in the awful days after Phoebe's initial stroke, her mother had been in a coma for almost a week, and Rebecca had come to terms with losing her, in long hours at Phoebe's bedside that had felt like a losing fight in a stormy sea. Slipping beneath the tumult at last into the green dim quiet below had been, unforeseeably, a kind of peace. But then Phoebe had surfaced, gloriously, and though she was clearly not entirely herself, both physically and mentally, there had been at least the hope of eventual recovery, the program and discipline of working for that. Something to *do* that would make things better. A new routine, a viable condition.

Lately, though, there seemed to be no way around the increasingly obvious fact that Phoebe's recovery had peaked. Her nearest approach to her former self had been around the time of the wedding: there had been so much in the planning and arranging of the event that fed and strengthened the Phoebe of old, so much in the way of meaning and style and fine points that only Phoebe could do, and she had risen to the occasion joyfully and energetically. But in retrospect, that surge of approximate normality seemed like the high point of a tide; even when she came back from the honeymoon, after a mere week away, Rebecca had known that her mother had regressed. Physically, Phoebe was still making progress; she was walking better and farther, and her hand-eye coordination, while not sharp, had gotten good enough for the needlepoint phase to begin. But her mind was going. Her beautiful mind. Her mother, too often now, was gone, was simply and truly not there, was somewhere else; and Rebecca had come to be terrified of this stranger in her mother's body, this empty echo of Phoebe that summoned up all the old instant and deep emotions and responses and yet was not quite Phoebe. If it had been her mother taking off like that today, scaring everyone to death, Rebecca could have been furious with her. But she had felt no anger when Mike finally brought Phoebe back from her escapade. She had felt only a shudder of dread and despair, meeting eyes that were her mother's eyes, without her mother behind them.

"Are you okay, Becca?"

It was Rory, with a fresh beer. Rebecca looked down at the still-full, now-warm beer in her hand. Across the room, Chelsea and Zoe's parents were in an animated conversation about Central America, exchanging funny travel stories. Rory, unprecedentedly, had been acting as the de facto host and had even brought out chips and salsa and a plate of cheese. Life, against all odds, went on just fine without her for the moment; and perhaps because it so demonstrably did, Rebecca began to cry.

Rory immediately took her arm and led her out before anyone else noticed, through the kitchen and onto the back porch. The fog had rolled in, a cold pall on the afternoon. Below them, everything in Phoebe's once-hopeful little garden was dead except for the indestructible poppies and a few sad-looking zucchini plants. Rebecca put her face into Rory's chest and sobbed. He just patted her back and let her cry, without saying anything stupid, for which she was intensely grateful. He smelled like soccer, and like Stu-J, and like fifteen years of her life. It was all just too damn sad and strange.

Inside the house, the doorbell rang—the pizza guy, Rebecca realized. Shit. She straightened, to try to get herself together to go deal with that.

"It's okay, Chelsea's got it," Rory said.

"But the money—"

"It's covered, Becca," Rory said gently, which for some reason just made her begin to cry again. He'd never before been the one who paid for the pizza.

The first one to bed always lit the candle, and the last one to bed turned out the lamp. It was a ritual that had begun the second night Rebecca and Mike had slept together. On their first—candleless—night together, Rebecca had insisted on turning off the lamp; she was self-conscious about her body; there was no going back once you'd had a baby and breastfed. She felt that she would do, especially for a guy who hadn't had sex for over twenty years, but she didn't want to dwell on it. It had led to a brief comedy sequence: Mike had clicked the lamp back on, she'd clicked it off again, back and forth a couple of times, like two kids. Rebecca had finally gotten him to stop by saying the light was just too harsh. The next morning she'd succumbed unexpectedly to a sort of panic attack that had nothing to do with the lamp, a backlash in the cold light of day, and the relationship had gone into the crapper for weeks. But when they'd finally worked it through and come back together, the next time they got into bed together Mike had brought a candle, and he lit it, pointedly, when she turned the lamp off. A gentle light, as he noted with a smile. Rebecca had just been grateful to see his face; and anyway, she figured, he'd had plenty of time to bolt by then on an informed basis, if he had really required exceptionally perky breasts.

The tradition had seen them through quite a bit by now, and Rebecca had come to love the candlelight, not only because it meant that Mike loved to see her just the way she was, which was incredibly liberating once you began to actually believe it, but also because the light just felt holy to her. It made the end of the day into a kind of prayer, whether they made love or just lay in each other's arms and chewed over the day's portion of craziness; and there was that beautiful little puff of "Amen" when they blew the candle out and settled in to sleep.

Tonight, though, as Rebecca lay in bed while Mike brushed his teeth, the lighting of the candle just seemed . . . hokey. Empty, a forced cheer; a form of denial, even. She left it unlit, for the first time in their relationship, realizing as she did so that she was feeling alienated from Mike, was very close to being angry with him. It felt like they had somehow ended up on different sides of a crucial issue. Mike was almost eerily easy with Phoebe's madness. He could go from the Eisenhower administration to whether there were seagulls in purgatory to what kind of tea Phoebe wanted without missing a beat. Rebecca couldn't help envying his rapport with her mother, but she suspected that he was probably making Phoebe worse by humoring her like that. What Phoebe needed was better meds, clearly, closer supervision, unfortunately, and reality checks. It was painful, yes, but what was the alternative? Was it too much, to want your mother to be sane?

Mike came out of the bathroom and crossed to the bed, pausing as usual beside it to click off the lamp. Rebecca could feel his surprise, half a heartbeat of hesitation, as the room fell into darkness. And she felt a surge of something like grief, because the world was winning, after all, it was finally starting to wear them down. Like a storm, like a tide, like the thousand relentless things that battered beauty until it succumbed. The terrible world was stronger than their love.

Mike fumbled briefly in the dark and found the matches, lit one and got the candle going, then slipped into bed beside her, and their bodies found each other. His skin felt like home and the warm light felt holy. Just like that. Rebecca felt the truth of him, and of the two of them; and her lungs relaxed and took a breath. It seemed like she hadn't breathed in days.

"I didn't forget," she said. It felt like a confession, like something she had to get off her chest.

"I think maybe you did," Mike said.

If there had been a trace of smugness or blame in it, they would have had real trouble, but Rebecca knew what he meant. He was talking not about the candle, but about what the candle meant, of the difficulty, of the near impossibility, of remembering your real, best self, in the midst of the world's crush.

She had a flash of memory, of the evening Mike had proposed. They had been sitting under a plum tree outside Grace Cathedral, right after Bonnie's wedding there, and Mary Martha had been running through the labyrinth. The evening had been one of San Francisco's rare balmy treasures, the sunset bathing the cathedral towers in sweet rose gold. Rebecca had felt, that night, a peace so deep, a love so real, that it seemed there was no going back, that the world and her self must be forever transformed in its light. It was something she had felt at Phoebe's hospital bedside as well, something she had sworn to herself then that she would not lose sight of, would not forget, ever again. But she had, of course. Almost instantly, at the first honk of a horn out on the street, the first blown fuse, the first alarm clock going off after a short night's sleep.

They had talked that night about how easy it was to lose sight of that peace. Mike had told her about a print in the monastery library, a copy of Filippo Lippi's painting of St. Augustine beholding the Trinity in a vision: sitting at his desk with an inkpot and a scroll on his knee, gazing raptly at a three-faced sun shining above him ... with three arrows sticking out of his heart.

Those moments of rapturous union came and went, Mike had said, by God's grace, and to the daily self they seemed in retrospect unreal, if recalled at all; but the arrows, by God's grace, stayed. It was the arrows, he said, that pain in the heart, that wound to the daily self, that helped you remember what your soul had always known.

Rebecca said now, thinking of those arrows, "It's weird, but I really didn't see this Phoebe stuff coming. Maybe I'm a Pollyanna after all, but once we had made it through the hospital time and gotten her home, I had pictured a sunset decade of mild decline, cooking soups and gardening together, doing watercolors by lakes with ducks, talking about profound things and debriefing her on that amazing life of hers. Watching Mary Martha grow up. And then she could die quietly in her bed, like a candle going out, with me holding her hand."

"It may happen yet," Mike said.

"You know that's not true."

"Maybe I'm a bigger Pollyanna than you." He hesitated, then conceded, "She does seem to believe herself that she's on a faster track out."

"Do you think she's ... "

Mike waited, then prompted gently, "Suicidal?"

Rebecca began, quietly, to cry. The word struck her as obscene, in conjunction with her mother. But it was what she had been asking.

Mike drew her closer. "I don't think she is, in a strict sense," he said, after a moment. "But I think she expected to die on that beach today."

They were silent for a time. The candle flickered in its cup at the touch of a draft, then settled again.

"She said that she was waiting for your father," Mike said.

"Oh, God. Really?"

"Yes."

"She really believes he's alive? And coming for her?"

"He has a boat," Mike said.

Rebecca's heart ached. Her father's boat had been one of the joys of her parents' life, and of her own childhood; so many of her sweetest memories were of the family out on the water. If she were Phoebe, and losing it, she would want that boat to come for her too. And she realized that she could forgive Mike for egging her mother on, after all. She was just glad that Phoebe had someone she could talk to, on that cold beach, waiting for her dead husband to take her to heaven, or New Jersey.

She said, "When I'm on my way out, will you come in a boat for me?"

"Sure," Mike said. "I may have to steal one, though."

They lay quietly together for a time, and then Rebecca said, "This is not the drama that I wanted for us, Mike. When we married. I thought maybe we'd have to have a bunch of theatrical fights about God, or the practicality of the New Testament in an Old Testament world, or something like that. Instead, we're moving toward having to change my mother's diapers."

"If it's not one thing, it's another," he said. "Love is still just love."

It was true enough, she thought, to go to sleep on. She eased back and leaned over to blow the candle out, then settled back into the warmth of his arms.

"I love you," she said. "I love you. I love you."

"I love love you you," he said.

It was a Mary Martha-ism, and a touch of their private silliness, a quiet way of saying that life went on and tomorrow was another day. Rebecca smiled into her husband's chest, breathing in the comfort of him, and closed her eyes. The good-night, at this point in their marriage, was implied.

Chapter Ten

It is of the Lord's mercies that we are not consumed;
his compassions fail not.
They are new every morning: great is Thy faithfulness.

LAMENTATIONS 3:22–23

A s the hart panteth after the water brooks, so panteth my soul after Thee, O Lord.

The man's name was Tony, though no one had called him that for years. His street name had been Sly, and it had fit his manner. But his slyness had run its course now, his hustling had come to nothing, and he wanted, fiercely and abruptly, to be called by his given name. It was the first sign of understanding what was happening to him that Mike had seen in the two weeks he had known the man. The rest had been attitude, posture, and existential bluster.

It was one of the hard ones. Tony's lungs were almost gone, and what was left of them could not pump strongly enough to fight the fluid accumulating in them, to surface from the slow drowning that made every breath a gurgling struggle. But the physical agony was not the worst of it. He was in and out of consciousness, and when he was awake his terror was like an electric wire with its insulation shredded, a visceral current arcing across the space between the two men so that Mike felt every jolt and shock of it in his own nerves.

Dougherty had called Mike in the night before, just after midnight; Tony had been asking for him. It had been clear to all of them then that Tony was moving into his endgame. But sixteen hours later the man fought on. Every pant was its own painful adventure, a new labor sixteen times a minute. He would stop breathing sometimes now, for fifteen, twenty, thirty unnerving seconds, and Mike would be sure he was gone. But then with a shudder Tony's chest would heave back into action, a violent, liquid gasp that seemed even more painful after the quiet of the pause, and he would resume the gurgling, metronomic panting.

My soul thirsteth for God, for the living God: when shall I come and appear before Thee?

The doctor had already been in and had just shaken his head quietly at Mike and slipped away. Tony had a clicker in his hand, a single button to activate the morphine pump, but he had refused to use it. Like embracing his given name, it was a belated, furious, and somewhat incomprehensible insistence: a couple clicks, they all knew, and he was gone. This fight could lead nowhere but defeat; the pain and terror gained him nothing but a few more minutes or hours of more terror and pain. But apparently Tony had decided that it was here that he would make his stand.

The floor nurse, Anita, had made sure the IV morphine bag was hung and working at the start of her shift and had since avoided the room, as if Tony's palpable agony were communicable. She was a good nurse too: Mike had seen her in action half a dozen times already, moving straight into the face of suffering, always doing what she could. But this was a bad one, there was nothing to do but ride it down, and Anita was keeping herself busy elsewhere with people she could still do something for.

Mike himself had long since given up trying to find the meaning. Why he was here and what it meant, what Tony needed and what he or anyone could give this soul in the hour of need, what inscrutable Love asked of any of them here, it had all been used up long since. Mike wasn't even sure Tony knew he was there anymore; the dying man had met his eyes only once in the last hour, pointing to his dry tongue, which Mike had wetted with a glycerin swab dipped in water, trying not to flinch from Tony's breath, which smelled like wind from an opened grave.

Deep calleth unto deep at the noise of Thy waterspouts; all Thy waves and billows have gone over me.

Tony's free left hand fluttered, some kind of request. Mike swabbed his tongue again, but that wasn't it, and after a moment's hesitation Mike did the only other thing he could see to do, which was take the man's hand in his. It appeared that was what Tony had wanted; his grip tightened on Mike's hand instantly, with surprising strength.

They sat like that, with the shallow ragged panting keeping the only time. Tony's eyes were closed now, as if breathing itself required all his concentration.

And then, abruptly, his breathing stopped again, though his grip stayed steady. Mike sat still in the room's sudden stillness and prayed silently, knowing it took him about fifteen seconds to say an internal Hail Mary. He was well into his third prayer when Tony's body shuddered through its entire length and his claw grip on Mike's hand clenched to the point of pain, and still no breath came, just his mouth gaping and groping as if for a word; and then his chest lifted as if a band had snapped and his breath came as a gasp, and he was panting again.

Tony's eyes opened and his gaze found Mike's at once, in clear focus.

"Sur-prised ... " he said, between breaths.

"Surprised?"

"Every time ... I in-hale."

"So am I, to tell you the truth," Mike said.

"The truth," said Tony, who had spent so much of his life lying. He smiled. "I love ... the truth."

His eyes closed again and he resumed his steady panting, somehow without urgency now; and ten minutes later, when the next apnea came, he was still smiling, and his hand in Mike's turned gentle.

Why art thou cast down, O my soul? And why art thou disquieted within me? Hope thou in God: for I shall yet praise him, who is the health of my countenance, and my God.

You never knew, Mike thought, saying his Hail Marys silently; and then, after the fifth one, aloud, turning the rosary beads in his own free hand. Even going in, you never knew. And he knew less with every death.

R ebecca was astonished at how well she remembered her father's boat, once she began painting it. She had begun with only the vaguest image, but she found that it didn't matter so much what had stayed in her mind's eye. As a girl, she had spent so many winter weekends in the boathouse with her father, scraping barnacles and repainting the hull, that her hands could still feel the shape of the bow, the dip to the shallow keel, the long slide along the graceful flanks to the stern. It had been years before she realized that the off-season maintenance work was supposed to be tedious. All she had known then was how wonderful it was to be with her father in the chilly boathouse, with a thermos of coffee for him and a thermos of hot chocolate for her. He would sing sailing songs in a funny accent; Rebecca could still recall most of the words to "Way-Hey and Up She Rises." John Martin had actually had a hornpipe, and sometimes the two of them would dance absurd jigs on the cold concrete floor.

She had her easel set up in the dining room, or her office, or whatever it really was these days. She hadn't done any productive work for actual pay in weeks, so maybe it was just a studio now. Phoebe sat across from her in the big easy chair they had moved into the room, laboring in her slow and dreamy way over the eternal needlepoint, pausing over every stitch as if reenvisioning the entire pattern anew. Mary Martha was sprawled contentedly on the floor at Phoebe's feet, working on a drawing of her own.

It was a gorgeous scene, Rebecca thought, the three of them, like something out of *Little Women* or a domestic tableau by Vermeer, lit with a light like the gleam off pearls.

"What is that you're drawing, Mary Martha?" she asked.

"I'm copying Gran-Gran's needlepoint."

"Ah." Rebecca could usually recognize her daughter's subjects at once; Mary Martha was really quite good, and getting better all the time. For months now she'd been drawing unnervingly vivid pictures of the stations of the cross for her first communion class; their refrigerator, still in the living room, was covered with scene after scene of misery and holy gore. But this picture was just a bunch of dots and colored dashes; it looked like something by Klee, in a particularly austere mood. Rebecca hesitated, looking for something supportive to say but not sure exactly what. Maybe her daughter was going abstract on her. Or maybe she was just feeling goofy.

Phoebe had craned her neck to peer at her granddaughter's work too.

"Perfect," she said, and Mary Martha beamed and went back to work.

Rebecca gave her mother a baffled glance, suspecting that Phoebe was cheating somehow. Or maybe it was just that after your brain had deteriorated a certain amount, *everything* looked perfect. Phoebe met her eyes with a smile that said she knew exactly what Rebecca was thinking, then held up her needle-point to show Rebecca the back of it. It was the pattern of stitches on the underside that Mary Martha was drawing.

Rebecca didn't know whether to be more impressed with Mary Martha for doing that or with her mother for knowing it was happening. In any case, it was humbling. It made her wonder what else she was missing.

The phone rang just then, and they all just looked at it. They'd gotten out of the habit of answering the phone recently, to a comical extent. It had started with Mike, who never touched a ringing telephone unless he was pretty sure someone was literally dying. Phoebe had made a point of answering phones for a while after her first stroke, more out of noblesse oblige than anything else, but she had eventually decided they weren't worth the trouble. Mary Martha had stepped into the breach for a while and answered every call, but that had lost its novelty long since and now she tended to just go on with her business.

Rebecca had always answered the phone slavishly, as a mother and a daughter and a wife and a woman trying to get a business off the ground. But she had no jobs in progress right now, and hadn't for weeks, and so whenever she knew where Mary Martha, Mike, and Phoebe were, she too just let it ring.

The phone rang again, and then the answering machine kicked in. It was Jeff Burgess, something about a job. Rebecca hesitated for a long moment, then picked up.

"Hey," she said.

"You need a secretary, woman," Jeff said. "You're harder to get hold of lately than a greased pig."

"Well, you know how it is. One thing after another."

"Yeah, well, I've got a couple more things for you, if you want 'em."

"Graphics jobs?"

"Don't sound so thrilled," Jeff said dryly.

"Sorry. Big or small?"

"Medium."

Which meant enormous, of course. Rebecca looked at her mother and her daughter, both of them absorbed in their work. Mary Martha with her tongue out in concentration looked just like Rory, which was still touching somehow after all these years. Phoebe looked beautiful, serene, and oddly poised, like an autumn leaf leaking its last bit of color before it fell. It was exactly how Rebecca had pictured her life at its best, at various hopeful times; and, she knew, if her mother hadn't been hell-bent on dying, it was probably something that would never have happened at all, something that would have been lost in the daily scramble of things you just did and did and did because they were so immediate and obvious and apparently pressing, until something finally happened to make you realize they hadn't mattered at all and that you'd wasted all that precious time. Getting and spending: it was amazing, Rebecca thought, what it took to bring that heedless process to a halt. She could only be grateful, at this moment, that something had. They'd pay the mortgage somehow.

She said, "Thanks, Jeff, but I think I'm going to have to pass on these."

"What? You've got somebody else subbing you stuff? You're really that overloaded?"

"No, not really. I'm just in, uh, a lull, of sorts. A contemplative phase."

"Use it or lose it, Bec," Jeff said, a bit severely.

"Ain't it the truth," Rebecca said.

She hung up the phone and got back to her painting. She was having a wonderful time with the blues. As a teenager, she had adored the work of Caspar David Friedrich, the sweeping romance of his sacred-feeling landscapes, and this felt a bit like that, the small boat dwarfed by an immensity of holy sea and sky.

"Is that Grandpa driving the boat?" Mary Martha asked.

"Yes."

"Aren't you going to put Gran-Gran on it too?"

Rebecca hesitated, thinking, Honey, there is no *way* I'm letting your grandmother onto this boat. She glanced across at Phoebe and saw at once that her mother understood her perfectly. It was almost funny. Phoebe hardly ever talked anymore, and often when she did the sentences petered out for lack of the next word, or she simply didn't make enough sense to keep a conversation going with anyone but Mike, who didn't necessarily require sense, somehow. But as Phoebe had spoken less and less, Rebecca had come to realize how often the mother she missed so much was still there. She had been so wigged out by Phoebe's dementia that she hadn't been able to see past it. But a look like this was the best of their relationship, had always been the best: the shared understanding, the mutual acknowledgment of a tricky truth, and the dry humor. Her mother got her as few people did, as no one ever really had but Mike, and loved her anyway.

Rebecca said, "Sometimes Grandpa went out by himself."

"Didn't he get lonely?"

Rebecca looked at her mother again, a frank appeal for help. And Phoebe said obligingly, in one of those bursts of sweet lucidity that made Rebecca suspect her mother might live for years still, like an increasingly feeble and enigmatic sphinx, "No, sweetie, your grandfather always felt like he was with God, on the boat."

T he much-deferred dinner at the Schofields' finally caught up with them that Friday night: it was Bonnie's fortieth birthday, the big 4–0, and more or less unmissable. Rebecca began to have inklings of disaster when Bonnie called three times during the day with excited little details, confidings, and last-minute tasks and requests; she was so up for the event that it would have been nerve-racking even for a social optimist, which Rebecca was not. She tried to call Mike at work, to warn him that the thing was acquiring an outsized momentum, but his cell phone was turned off, which meant that whoever had been dying the night before was still dying. She felt incredibly petty, but she could not help but hope that whoever it was, God bless him and *requiescat in pacem,* he moved on to his eternal rest in time for Mike to get home and get a shower and some downtime before the party.

When Mike did finally get home, just after six, he looked as exhausted as Rebecca had ever seen him, and her sense of impending calamity sharpened. He gave her a kiss, not a hello-honey-I'm-home peck but a conspicuously gentle, prolonged, and searching kiss, like a man coming home from time at sea. Rebecca didn't have the heart to tell him before he got his land legs back that he had more work to do that evening, and in any case Mary Martha ran in just then as she always did when Mike got home and he immediately put on a good face for her. He lifted her up onto his lap, and the two of them bumped and nuzzled and talked about her day for about ten minutes with every appearance of sweet normality. If anything, Mike was exceptionally tender with her; but when Mary Martha went back up to her room, he grabbed a beer at once and, with a rueful tilt of his head inviting Rebecca to follow, went straight out to the back porch. Not good, she knew: he almost never smoked when Mary Martha was around and awake. She poured herself a glass of wine and went out after him.

He already had a cigarette lit when she sat down beside him on the top step. Rebecca glanced back over her shoulder at Mary Martha's bedroom window and was relieved to see no sign of her daughter. When Mary Martha caught Mike smoking, she often heaved her window open and started shouting grisly antismoking facts down at him. Rebecca suspected that even if it had not yet stopped Mike, a number of the neighbors might have quit by now.

Mike took her hand as she sat down. The evening was clear, the sun still well above the ocean. They sat quietly for a time. Mike's silence was almost palpable, a distinct thing as real as an egg. He was not morose but definitely brooding, keeping that egg of silence warm, cradling it at the heart of his attention.

A mockingbird swooped across the backyard, lit in a treetop next door, and launched into a prolonged and vigorous medley.

"You tell 'em, buddy," Mike said.

It constituted an opening of sorts, and Rebecca took the opportunity to say, mock-brightly, "So, how was your day, honey?"

Mike shook his head and smiled, acknowledging the humor, but said nothing. He was often like this after a death, and Rebecca knew that it just took time. For a day or two or sometimes more, he would spend more time in the attic at prayer, or with Phoebe, talking their private underwater talk, or with Mary Martha, which clearly was simple and healing for him. The house often felt like a monastery at such times; Rebecca would find herself speaking in lowered tones, moving around more quietly, slowing down in general to the point where the telephone was jarring and the TV seemed like a nightmare in a box. She had wondered, when she married Mike, how he would adjust to the pace of the world, and at times she had feared—as she knew he had, and did—that the world's demands would somehow dilute or even defeat that thing in him that she loved so much, the inner stillness that so often startled her into her own best self, and the discipline and single-mindedness it took to cultivate that stillness. But what she had found was that in many ways Mike let the world, de facto, adjust to *him:* there were so many things he simply did not do, did not even seem to miss doing, that they not only were not distractions, it was as if they did not exist.

Like going to birthday parties. Rebecca was steeling herself to bring it up when Mike said, "How's Phoebe, today?"

"Good," Rebecca said. "I guess. She actually ate something at lunch. We only made it about five blocks on the walk, but she seemed okay with that." She hesitated, then said, "It's so weird. She's so at peace with everything right now, and I find myself getting sucked right into it."

Mike laughed.

"No, I'm serious," Rebecca said. "I mean, isn't it my responsibility to help her fight? And she hasn't got an ounce of fight left in her, it seems. I always thought that if anyone was going to rage, rage against the dying of the light, it would be my mother. But she seems to want to go out like a lamb."

"Phoebe's a lion," Mike said. "No matter how she stays or goes." He finished his beer and dropped his cigarette butt into the empty bottle. If the usual rhythm held, Rebecca knew, he would either get himself a second beer immediately or plead existential extremity and disappear into the attic for several hours to meditate on death and eternity.

Before he could do either, she took a breath and said, "Mike, it's Bonnie's birthday."

He caught her tone at once, and said, carefully, "Uh-huh."

"There's a party."

"Tonight?"

"Yes."

Mike groaned, frankly, and Rebecca saw him for a moment as just a guy, her guy, tired, grumpy, and recalcitrant. It was actually a relief. She could deal with guys. No one knew how to deal with saints. If he was really a damn saint, or even trying to be, he should have stayed in the monastery where it was safe. The world was the world. St. Francis had hung out with lepers; the least Mike could do was go to a birthday party.

She said, steadily, "It's been on our calendar for a month." And, as he said nothing, "It's her *birthday*, Mike. My best friend. Her fortieth, a huge one, and she's as excited about it as a little girl."

This was shameless, she knew, the subtle equation with Mary Martha. But at least it let him know she was serious here.

Mike was silent for a long moment. His beer bottle twitched once in his hand, and she knew he had almost sipped at it before remembering it was empty. It was interesting, Rebecca thought: how long she had known him now, and how deeply, and yet she had no idea what he was going to say. This was new territory for them, a renegotiation of the marital-monastic charter.

"I'm not going to get any more beer tonight unless we go, am I?" Mike said at last.

Rebecca smiled, trying not to look smug, and shook her head.

"Well, then," Mike said. "I guess we should bring balloons."

•   •   •

The Schofields' home was decked out with streamers, "The Big Four-Oh!" banners, and, inexplicably, three lava lamps. A disco ball spun lopsidedly from the living room ceiling, where several couples were boogeying languidly to a CD of *Greatest Love Songs of the 80s.* The bulk of the crowd was in the den, where Bob stood behind a bar mixing Bonnie Bombs, the drink *de soir,* a potent mix of vodka, cherry schnapps, cranberry juice, a touch of tonic water for fizz, and more vodka. He waved gaily as Rebecca and Mike came in and handed them two premade drinks in big plastic cups. Mike took one sip of his, set it down discreetly, and slipped away to try to find a beer. He was trailing a large red and yellow balloon that said Happy Anniversary, which was all they had been able to find on short notice at Andronico's on the drive over, and he seemed reconciled to his fate. Rebecca just hoped he would last until the cake was cut and the presents opened. She had told him he could smoke as much as he wanted and she wouldn't tell Mary Martha.

Bonnie was nowhere to be seen at first. Rebecca found her at last in the kitchen, chopping asparagus and looking gloomy.

"What's wrong, birthday girl?" Rebecca said, after giving her a hug.

"Nothing."

"Hey, sweetheart, it's me."

Bonnie glanced at the door; they were alone for the moment. She said, "Not a big deal, really. Just a little tiff."

"With Bob?"

"He's been stressed out about the pasta. I mean, like, *snappy.*" Bonnie shook her head at herself. "What a stupid thing to fight about, huh?"

"Yeah," Rebecca said. "Mike and I only fight about really important things, like the wording of the Nicene Creed, and whether he puts the toilet seat down."

"I told him, Bob, it's just *noodles.* But it's not just noodles to him, it's—shit, I don't know. Art. *Cuisine.*" She checked again for privacy, then leaned closer to confide, "Becca, I hate to say it, but he can be such an *ass* sometimes."

Rebecca resisted an urge to look at her watch. Fourteen months, two weeks, six days, and eight hours, more or less, since Bonnie and Bob had first met at a beach party in Marin the previous summer, and this was the first time Bonnie had ever intimated that Bob might be anything less than spectacularly wonderful. Not a bad run, as honeymoons went; but it was definitely a relief that the moratorium on criticism might be ending.

"*Bob?*" she said, with an over-the-top incredulity that was its own comment.

Bonnie smiled in wry concession, as if to say, Yeah, yeah, don't rub it in. It was as if she had known all along that Bob's exemption would eventually expire.

Rebecca said, offering tit for tat, "At least he's throwing himself into it. Mike is here by the skin of his teeth."

"I'm amazed that he showed up at all," Bonnie said, mildly enough. "I thought you guys were never going to get over here."

Rebecca got her point: Bob wasn't the only one who'd been enjoying a waiver of sorts. She said, "It really hasn't been personal. The guy barely functions after dark. We chant vespers right after dinner and go to bed."

Bonnie shook her head sympathetically. "We watch *Seinfeld, ER,* and the eleven o'clock news. God forbid we should fall asleep without knowing tomorrow's weather."

"Ain't married life grand?"

"On the whole," Bonnie allowed, and they smiled at each other. "Oh, hey, speaking of married life—did you see today's *Chronicle?*"

"I haven't had a minute. It seems like all I do anymore is hang out with Phoebe."

"Well, your ex is a hero." Bonnie crossed to the kitchen table and found the newspaper. "See?"

It was the local section, and there was a big picture of Rory and three adorable kids above the fold. He had apparently saved each of their lives in the last month or so, and the city had given him a medal.

"Wow," Rebecca said. "I hope his parole officer sees this." But she realized that beyond her deeply ingrained disinclination to get too built up about anything positive Rory did, she was actually pleased, and even vaguely proud. Somehow, against all odds, she and Rory were on the same team at this point in their lives. Maybe even for the first time. She was sincerely rooting for the father of her daughter. How strange, that that should be a revelation.

"Do you want that copy?" Bonnie asked.

"Yes, thanks. Mary Martha will be thrilled." Rebecca shook her head. "Bonnie, it's so weird. Mike is more like Rory than I ever imagined he would be, and Rory is like God-knows-who now. Phoebe is talking about dying like it's a trip to the store. I can't pay our health insurance. And yet somehow, something in me is telling me it's all okay."

"Your deep self," Bonnie said knowledgeably.

"Maybe. Hopefully. But what if my deep self is just clueless?"

Bonnie laughed and went back to the counter, where she picked up her knife, took a sip of her wine, and got back to work. Rebecca took a matching sip of her Bonnie Bomb, realized that it was terrible, and dumped the drink down the sink. Bonnie's glass of wine was right there, and she picked it up to get the taste of the sugar and vodka out of her mouth and realized that Bonnie's wine was grape juice.

Her brain skipped a beat, and then another. Bonnie was looking at her with an odd half smile, a bit expectantly, as if it were a test of some sort.

Rebecca said slowly, "Okay, either you've gone on the wagon or … "

"Or," Bonnie said.

"*Really?*"

Bonnie nodded happily. Rebecca threw her arms around her. "Oh, my God, sweetheart! This is fantastic!"

"Fantastic hardly even begins to cover it," Bonnie said.

Rebecca released her and peered frankly at her belly. Bonnie laughed. "It's only at about five weeks, Becca."

"The, uh, technical solutions worked?"

"We managed it the old-fashioned way, actually."

"That's best of all."

"Yeah," Bonnie said. She was glowing, her gloom long gone. "Bob's going to announce it tonight, I'm afraid. I'd rather wait for a month or two. I mean, what if I lose it?"

"I didn't tell anyone about Mary Martha until I was so far along that store clerks were commenting on it. Tell Bob to keep his big mouth shut."

"I did," Bonnie said. "You know Bob."

Their eyes met. Rebecca felt a warm rush of joy. The Stepford Bonnie was definitely gone. Her best friend was really back.

"Boys will be boys," she said.

"You got that right," Bonnie said. "I'm chopping the asparagus at my own damned birthday party."

The party was a good-natured success, despite the rubberiness of Bob's rotini. The cocktail hour's generous portions of Bonnie Bombs had left everyone in a receptive mood in any case. Rebecca noticed that Mike even had seconds on the noodles—rather heroically, she thought—which clearly pleased Bob. Rebecca kept one ear tuned to the two men's conversation, a bit uneasily, as Bob had a tendency to bait people sometimes, but they spent most of the dinner talking about the Giants. Mike had somehow maintained a passable fluency in sports talk despite going twenty years without seeing a

World Series or Super Bowl. Bob had strong opinions about the Giants' bullpen; apparently they were misusing their middle relievers. Mike couldn't have agreed more.

Rebecca found herself talking with the other women about the fact that she was remodeling her kitchen. She hadn't even realized that was what she was doing until Bonnie brought it up, but it sounded so wonderfully suburban and appeared to delight everyone, and it led into all manner of shared sagas and ordeals. One of the women even wanted the name of her contractor, but fortunately just then Bob stood up and tapped his knife on his glass.

The room fell silent, and Bob made a long and lovely toast to the birthday girl, to much applause, and followed it up with an announcement of the pregnancy, to gleeful cheers. Bonnie blushed prettily through it all, though she managed to roll her eyes briefly at Rebecca at one point, below the general radar. The cake was brought in with forty actual candles burning, and Bonnie blew them out with much exaggerated huffing and puffing, to more cheers and jokes about Lamaze breathing.

As the cake was cut into pieces and distributed, people wandered off with them to spots around the house to lounge and chat, the party moving naturally into a more diffuse winddown stage. Rebecca began to help clear the table. She had more or less relaxed about Mike and Bob, but as she was stacking plates to haul away she realized that the tenor of conversation at that end of the table had changed. Bob was talking about genes for some reason, making some complicated case about the difference between men and women, with a certain amount of uncontextual passion. Mike was nodding, apparently humoring him, but when his eye briefly met Rebecca's his look clearly said, I love you and wish to please but I'm leaving soon whether you do or not.

Bonnie had appeared at the kitchen door, also alerted by the music of the conversation. Rebecca took her stack of plates to the kitchen and paused beside her friend.

"Don't mind Bob," Bonnie said. "He just read some book about selfish genes and he's a little fired up. A chicken is just the egg's way of making another egg, that sort of thing. Men want harems, women want a good provider, but we're all just here to reproduce."

"I think Mike just hit his bedtime."

"He's been so sweet. Get him out of here before he decides he never wants to come back."

"You're okay with the cleanup?"

"It's my birthday," Bonnie said. "Every woman in the place is already helping."

Rebecca put the plates into the dishwasher, but by the time she returned to the dining room, Bob had moved on to making a case that monasticism was unnatural, a subversion of the genes' agenda.

"You got out just in time," he told Mike cheerfully. "For twenty years, your genes were screaming in protest."

"I wondered what all that noise was during compline," Mike said.

"Bobby, lighten up," Bonnie said, moving in from the kitchen door.

"It's all in good fun, honey. Just an intellectual exercise." Bob turned back to Mike. "See, that's where Jesus missed it, in my opinion. All that Sermon on the Mount stuff, turn the other cheek, the meek shall inherit the earth, sure, it's all great, in theory, but it flies in the face of the truth of the genes. It's an evolutionary, uh, aberration."

"Not to mention getting nailed to a cross," Mike said.

"Exactly! Before having any children! Talk about a selection event!"

"Would you like some coffee, Mike?" Bonnie asked.

"Thanks, no, Bonnie." Mike glanced at his watch, and then at Rebecca. "Actually, I think we—"

"I mean, what if I tried to take your woman?" Bob said.

"*Bob!*" Bonnie said.

"It's just a scenario, honey. To make a point." And, to Mike, "Come on, Brother Michael. I've grabbed Rebecca's hair and I'm dragging her off. What would you do, as a Christian?"

"For God's sake, Bob, knock it off," Bonnie said. "Mike, just ignore him."

"It's okay," Mike said. "But it *is* getting late—"

"I'm truly interested," Bob said. "Humor me, for a minute. I really want to know what you would do."

Mike arched an eyebrow at Rebecca, who shrugged: his call. He turned back to Bob. "Well, assuming Rebecca hasn't already broken your arm herself, I would say, 'Bob, thank you for a lovely evening, but you've had too much to drink. Let go of Rebecca's hair.'"

"I *have* had too much to drink!" Bob persisted. "That's the *point*. My genes are running the show. So I ignore you, and just keep dragging her away. What then?"

Bonnie would have stepped in at that point and perhaps hauled Bob himself off by the hair, but Rebecca put a hand on her friend's arm to stop her. She was interested in the answer, she realized. Maybe it was perverse, maybe it was her own genes assessing her partner's fitness. Who knew? But she wanted to hear what Mike would say.

Mike had noted Rebecca holding off Bonnie, and he gave her an amused look. "Well, obviously the dynamics would be complex, if you tried to haul Rebecca off to your cave," he said to Bob.

"No, no complexity. It's Malthusian, it's the jungle, my genes against yours."

"The complexity is inevitable," Mike said. "My genes somehow led me to spend my prime breeding years grappling with the truths of the gospel, with the fact that Jesus said to resist not evil. To judge not, to love your enemies, and to render unto Caesar that which is Caesar's, and unto God that which is God's."

"I'm not talking about the overlay of Christian ego, I'm talking about your inner primate male," Bob said. "And I'm almost out the door with your woman, here, buddy."

"Well, assuming that Rebecca is not Caesar's, and that basic social decorum has truly and completely failed," Mike said, "I suppose that at that point my inner primate male would be forced to kick your sorry ass."

Something in his tone finally made Bob stop. There was a long beat of silence, and then Bonnie said, "Are you sure you guys don't want some coffee?"

"Thanks, no, I think we'll call it a night," Rebecca said.

"Would you really beat up Bob Schofield for me, honey?" she asked Mike that night, when they were safely in bed with the lamp out and the candle going.

"Sure," Mike said. "Though I think Bonnie might beat me to it, in practice."

Rebecca smiled. "She was great tonight, wasn't she? I hope she felt like she had a good birthday."

"Me too. I think she did."

"She's so happy about the baby. She's been wanting that so much."

"Maybe that's why Bob was so hot and heavy on the importance of the genes," Mike said. "He feels he's a reproductive success."

"I think Bob is basically just a victim of the last book he read. And he'd had a little too much wine. Bonnie said he was stressed out beforehand about the pasta."

"No one wants to feel their rotini is inadequate," Mike said.

They lay quietly for a moment in each other's arms. Rebecca was just beginning to consider blowing out the candle when Mike said, "Are *your* genes screaming anything?"

"What?" Rebecca said.

"What Bob was saying about the agenda of the genes. The egg using the chicken to make more eggs. Do you feel that?"

Rebecca felt a surge of adrenaline, like sudden fire in her nerves. But she said, lightly enough, "Am I the chicken or the egg, here?"

"You know what I mean," Mike said. "Do you want to have a kid?"

"I already *have* a kid," Rebecca said; and, hearing the obfuscation in that, "Mike, I love our life. Exactly as it is. I love you, exactly as you are."

"Me too. But that doesn't answer my question."

"Is this because of Bonnie? You're afraid I feel left out of the baby bonanza? Or did Bob just get to you, with all that chest thumping about breeding?"

"I'm just asking," Mike said.

"Do I want to have a child? You mean, *your* child? Our child?"

"Yes."

"You mean, do I want to have another baby, with you, despite the fact that my mother is turning into a full-time job, I already can't keep up with my business, which is losing money, your job barely pays your bus fare, we already have Mary Martha, I'm almost forty years old, and you're a man who—how can I put this—treasures his quiet? His hours and hours of quiet? Which are a lot tougher to come by, to say the least, with a baby in the house."

"It's a yes-no question, Rebecca."

"Yes, then," she said. "Yes, truly. I would love that."

Mike was silent, for such a long time that Rebecca felt completely exposed; and when she could bear it no more, she said, "Why on earth did you ask *now?*"

"I don't know," he said. "I guess I felt like I was ready to."

"'But'?" she prompted, hearing it in his tone.

"But maybe I was only ready for the question," he said. "Not for the answer."

Chapter Eleven

He was divine, but He did not cling to His divinity;
He took the form of a servant, and became like us,
and was humbler yet, even to accepting death on a cross.

PHILIPPIANS 2:6–8

This is my last sunrise, Phoebe thought.

It was the first time in weeks that the fog had not been too thick to see the hills to the east. She sat on the top step in front of the house, her morning spot, and the sky was nothing but clear thin blue, and the light of the approaching sun made a halo in advance of itself above the dark line of the distant ridge. As if for all that time the fog submerging her at dawn had been the smoke from a fire burning dirty wood, and now everything was burned off but the cleanest fuel, and there was nothing but light and heat and the tempered blade of the pain, hard enough and sharp enough at last to cut through the world's cold grip without even a whisper of resistance.

What a gift, Phoebe thought, to have seen death coming from so far off. What a gift to have been wounded first and glimpsed it all, and given a reprieve, what a gift to have had time to learn to recognize the truth in the flame. She had been so sure the inscrutable smoke was meaning, and tried to read it, and that the inescapable pain was failure, and that its blade was something to fight with. But all the wrongness and phony hope had burned out of her, through the mercy of the fire, and all the need for it to be anything but what it was. There was nothing left but the blessing.

The edge of the sun cleared the ridge, and the light swelled and blossomed, showing the night for the passing thing it was. Phoebe blinked and lowered her gaze, her old eyes unable to stand it, head-on, even for a moment. But she could feel the new-born warmth.

No man shall see my face and live. But that wasn't true at all, except in ways that vomited clouds of smoke like the burning of dirty wood. If you waited it out, you saw right through it in the end. *I have seen Your face everywhere now, My God and my salvation,* Phoebe thought. *You can't fool me anymore. And this is my last dawn.*

T he daily walk had been getting shorter and shorter, not even reaching the first corner sometimes. Today Phoebe and Rebecca were only about five steps down the sidewalk in front of the house before Phoebe stopped.

"Are you all right, Mom?" Rebecca asked. Phoebe had that look of inscrutable absorption she often got now, attending to some pain or distress or vagueness within.

"I'm fine, sweetheart. Just a little on the watery side today."

"Shall we just go back and sit down for a bit?"

"That might be best," Phoebe conceded.

Rebecca nodded happily, relieved to not have to argue about it. Phoebe often insisted on forging on, even after she had broken a sweat. Rebecca took her mother's arm, and they made their slow way back up the sidewalk, and Phoebe for once didn't throw an elbow at her or try to shrug her off but let Rebecca help ease her down onto the step. Rebecca didn't know whether to be heartened by that or freaked out. But it was such a beautiful day, the first blue sky before noon in weeks, and she decided to just enjoy it.

When her mother was settled, Rebecca sat down beside her. They were quiet for a while. Sometimes now they still talked as they had always talked, girl talk and the daily flak, but more often they just floated along on a placid river of silence, broken by the occasional remark surfacing unpredictably from somewhere in Phoebe's depths like a fish going after a fly. Rebecca was finding herself much more comfortable lately, both with the conversational anomalies and with her mother's long periods of quiet.

"Is your husband all right?" Phoebe asked at last.

Rebecca considered. Mike was spending his Saturday morning off in the attic. This wasn't completely unusual; he often vanished into prayer for hours at a time, the way some men went fishing or drank, and not always at the most convenient moments; and one of his guys had died yesterday, after all. But Rebecca knew that he was freaked out about having finally broached the question of children. She suspected that she should have lied when he asked, but she wasn't sure she would know how to lie to Mike. When they had awakened that morning, slightly hungover, they had made gentle, mutually reassuring love; but at the crucial moment Mike had reached for a condom, an apology in his eyes. And afterward had fled into prayer.

Oh, well, Rebecca thought. The poor guy had to do something until the bars opened.

"Mike's fine," she said, deciding to just keep it simple.

"No, not Mike," Phoebe said. "The one who surfs."

"Rory?" Rebecca said, intrigued, and a little touched by the glimpse of her mother's inner processes. Once a husband, always a husband, apparently, in the depths of Phoebe's mind. "Rory's all right too."

"Good," Phoebe said. "I was so sure he would die."

"Only if he doesn't get that kitchen finished soon," Rebecca said.

They were silent again for a time, and then Phoebe offered, with an air of confiding and a certain rich satisfaction, "My husband's name is John."

"I know, Mom," Rebecca said, and took her mother's hand.

O *Lord, thou hast searched me and known me.*
It was not the crisis that Mike had expected. He had been prepared for the challenges of relationship, the inevitable trickiness of a marriage's emotional and practical

dance, to be the hard thing. But it turned out that the monastery had been extraordinarily good training for simply being decent with someone on a daily basis. It wasn't like taking the monastic vows made someone immune to being a pain in the ass. Mike had lived for years with prickly men hyperconscious of their elbow room in the choir stall, alive to violations of etiquette at doorways and in the halls, jealous of a hundred fine points of seniority and petty privilege. He'd fought with his abbot for decades, in a struggle to the death as savage and intimate as any marriage. And Mike knew he'd been no prize himself.

The thing was, spiritual practice did not erase the ego; most spiritual practice only refined it, made it subtler, cannier, and more noxious. And a monastery was not a dry county in the country of ego alcoholics; it was a brewery, a bar open twenty-four hours a day, a place not of escape from the ego but of immersion in it. You had to bottom out on the ego, had to come to know it for the poison that it was, whether you were in a monastery, a mansion, or a house in the Sunset. Rebecca was actually much easier to live with than most of the monks, and a dream compared to Abbot Hackley. She could be sharp as a razor, but at least she didn't think her moods, desires, and prejudices were the will of God, that she knew what was best for Mike's soul and had a divine mandate to impose it. She had a great, redeeming sense of humor, and she took him more or less as he came. He loved being married to Rebecca; it was a joy, down to the smallest details.

Thou knowest my downsitting and mine uprising, thou understand-est my thought afar off. Thou compassest my path and my lying down, and art acquainted with all my ways. There is not a word in my tongue, but, lo, O Lord, thou knowest it altogether.

He'd thought that being a stepfather might be beyond him somehow, but there was nothing in his relationship with Mary Martha that he did not love, from the precious predawn hours in church together to playing with her after work to getting thrown up on once in a while. He loved that girl; and there was nothing in his life as sweet as the happiness of her loving him back. Mike often felt sheepish, indeed, that he'd ever been afraid.

He'd also suspected that the challenge of dealing with Phoebe's debilitation and decline might overwhelm him, but there too he'd found only richness. The relationship with his mother-in-law felt like grace, like kinship even. He felt sometimes as if the two of them were a couple of ancient hermits, wandering in the vast desert of the mind, chuckling at the inscrutable ways of God. And Phoebe's courage and natural dignity, her humor and her faith touched him every day. Changing her diapers once in a while, tracking her down when she bolted for the ocean, even holding Rebecca in his arms while she sobbed on the nights when the imminent loss of her mother left nothing else to do, seemed like nothing in light of that.

No, Mike thought, he really hadn't seen it coming, quite like this: he loved his family. He had launched himself into the sky toward heaven all those years ago, a twenty-year flight like that of Icarus, higher and higher toward the pure life of the disembodied soul, until the sun melted the wax away from his greedy little mystical wings and he had all that time on the long fall from the heights of his imagined contemplative achievement to contemplate the actual idiocy of his targeted heaven and the realities of gravity. And now here he was, pinned like the tail on the donkey to the unmissable bull's-eye of the one true earth, just happy for a seat at the table in the little house on Thirty-eighth Avenue. Happy with the refrigerator in the living room, the stove in the hallway, and the health insurance unpaid. Happy to turn out the light at night and sink into Rebecca's arms, and happy to wake up in the morning and see her face and wonder what was next.

Such knowledge is too wonderful for me; it is high, I cannot attain it.

He even loved his work. That felt like a secret, almost, almost a kind of shame. He was weirdly attuned to the needs of the dying. It even made a kind of sense: he'd really prepared himself for little else during those years in prayer. Everything in him had fought, and everything in him had lost, again and again, led by failure after failure to the ultimate failure, to the eternal moment of mortal helplessness, to defeat and surrender. He did nothing with the dying but show up, and nothing for them but stay there, and in those hours with those men every temptation to do something heroic and holy and healing arose anew and died again. He held their hands and met their eyes and felt the terror and the pain, the futility and despair, as naked as the blade of a knife. There was nowhere to go and nothing to do, for him or for them; the world drained away like water from an emptying tub, and you saw what could only be seen when the world was gone.

Whither shall I go from thy spirit? Where shall I flee from thy presence? If I ascend up into heaven, thou art there; if I make my bed in hell, behold, thou art there.

No, Mike thought, he was at peace with dying, somehow. He had lived from death to death, had learned to find the vanishing point of peace, dragging a cross up a hill to the place of the skull. It even made a kind of deep sense to him, that the Word made flesh should find no place at last in the world but agony and failure and three days in the tomb. But what he apparently had yet to grasp, had yet to even begin to come to terms with, was the deeper mystery still, of the Word in a womb, of a night journey in winter to a place where animals slept, and an impossible birth, celebrated by shepherds and angels.

If I take the wings of the morning, and dwell in the uttermost parts of the sea—even there shall thy hand lead me, and thy right hand shall hold me.

The stairs to the attic creaked, and Mary Martha's head appeared above the gap in the floor. "Mike?"

"Hi, sweet pea. Are you all right?"

"Yes. But Mommy said to tell you it's time to take Gran-Gran to the hospital."

If I say, Surely the darkness shall cover me; even the night shall be light about me. Yea, the darkness hideth not from thee, but the night shineth as the day: the darkness and the light are both alike to thee.

What a clueless ass I am, Mike thought.

"Okay, sweetie," he said. "Let's go, then."

• • •

Rebecca had no idea how long it had taken her to notice. It might have been a minute or two, certainly not more than five minutes: a little spell of absorption in the painting, a meditation on how the sea met the sky, a play of green and gray and blue. It was long enough, she knew, that she would always feel the pain of not having noticed sooner. In any case, she had become aware at some point that it had been a while since Phoebe had spoken or moved, and she glanced over at her.

And had seen instantly that everything had changed. The slump was subtle, as was the slight sagging on the right side of her mother's face, but the overall effect was as obvious as a tire going flat. It made Rebecca realize how much her basic sense of her mother's appearance had altered, how quickly you grew accustomed to the most radical changes in someone. What seemed unbearable debilitation at first became the new norm in time, and you came to count on it in its turn and even, weirdly, to treasure it; and every further undoing was a new and painful loss. In the blink of an eye the speech-slurred, awkward, infinitely slow Phoebe of a moment before seemed like the shining image of a vanished heartiness. She had been dim and wan, and now was gray enough to make dim and wan seem bright; and her dreamy, drifting gaze, so unnerving for so long, had gone unnervingly vacant.

Rebecca sent Mary Martha upstairs to get Mike, trying for her daughter's sake to make it sound like it was time for a more or less normal doctor's appointment, and went to her mother's side. Phoebe made no perceptible response to her presence. Her breathing was shallow and quick but did not seemed threatened, and Rebecca decided not to call an ambulance. They would get to the hospital faster just taking her themselves, and Rebecca already knew that what the doctors did would depend on whether the stroke was hemorrhagic or ischemic, a bleeding from a weakened blood vessel or the clogging of a thinned one. The sooner they found out which, the sooner they could do something.

Rebecca was amazed by how composed she was. Phoebe's first stroke had freaked her out to the point of raging helplessness—she had harassed the doctors and badgered the nurses and walked around in a sort of furious haze for weeks. Most of the little slips and lapses along the path of her mother's decline, the lost words and unfinished sentences, the thoughts drifting into incoherence, the failures of bathroom skills and the getting lost in space and time on the way from one room to another, had pained her to despair. But now she just felt clear and calm and strangely tender. Apparently something in her had been preparing for this moment all along. The only time she cried, indeed, was when Mary Martha knelt at Phoebe's feet to get her shoes on for her and tied them perfectly, explaining the Bunny technique to her grandmother as she did, as patiently the hundredth time as she had the first.

•   •   •

t the hospital, Rebecca's sense of calm persisted. It was an unearthly quiet, a hush impervious to nightmare. They came in through the emergency room, and the dance of her mother's care proceeded with the brisk solemnity of ritual—the heartbreaking change of clothes, stripping her mother down to her frail body and dressing her in the green sad gown with the open back, the taking of the blood samples, the wheelchair run to the room with the tomblike MRI machine. Through it all Phoebe was obliging in a fashion, offering neither resistance nor help. She was quite gone, showing none of the distress she had always displayed when it was clear to her that she was out of it.

They put her in a bed in the ICU and drew the curtains to make a private space. The neurosurgeon came first and wanted to operate immediately; the blood-thinning medication Phoebe had been taking had led to a slow leakage of blood into her brain cavity, and the resultant pressure was cutting off the circulation. The cardiologist showed up next and said that there was no way Phoebe's blood pressure could be sustained at a high enough level for her to survive surgery, that her arteries would give way; the cerebrovascular guy, a moment later, agreed.

"How long will she survive, even if she has the surgery?" Rebecca asked the neurosurgeon.

He shrugged. "A week, maybe two, assuming we succeed in relieving the pressure. A month at most. But I'm afraid the brain damage is already enough to—"

"She wouldn't survive the surgery," the cardiologist said quietly. Rebecca glanced at the cerebrovascular doctor, who looked pained but nodded.

"How long without the surgery?" she said.

"I'm amazed she's alive now, to tell you the truth."

"Well, what *can* we do?"

"We can arrange for hospice care and make her as comfortable as possible," the cardiologist said. She had to give him credit; the man looked truly miserable. Both the other doctors nodded. They appeared relieved that the cardiologist was doing the talking.

Rebecca looked at Mike, who met her eyes quietly. Her call, completely. She had never loved him more. She said, "I hate to say it, but it sounds to me like we should just take her home."

"Yeah," he said.

They were all silent a moment.

"What is my prognosis?" Phoebe demanded suddenly from the bed.

They all looked at her in astonishment. Phoebe's eyes were open, all lights on. The doctors exchanged not-supposed-to-happen glances among themselves.

That's my mother, Rebecca thought. That's the one I know.

"Not good, Mom," she said. "There's not much they can do for you here right now. I mean, there's some kind of risky brain operation— "

"What would be the point, really?" Phoebe said, as if they were talking about whether to find a use for a loaf of week-old bread.

"That's sort of what we thought," Rebecca said. She hesitated, then said, "We're thinking about just taking you home."

Her mother looked at her sharply. "Home to die?"

Rebecca drew her breath in, looking for a way to soften it. But Mike said, "Yes."

"Well then," Phoebe said. "Let's get this show on the road."

Chapter Twelve

Father, into Your hands I commend my spirit.

LUKE 23:46

B ack at the house, they set Phoebe up in the master bed-room. Propped on three pillows, she had a view of the backyard and, across the housetops of the outer Sunset, the ocean. It seemed crucial to Rebecca that her mother have a view, though after her burst of lucidity at the hospital, Phoebe had settled into unresponsiveness again, her face a stolid mask without particular focus, her eyes closed much of the time and not particularly engaged when they were open. They'd gotten her dressed in her best flannel nightgown, the exquisite Victorian effect of which was somewhat diminished by the presence of the bedpan.

Mike called Anita, one of the nurses he worked with at the mission, and she arrived within half an hour. She was a sturdy woman in her midthirties, with henna red hair, sharp blue eyes, and an air of placid, no-nonsense efficiency. Rebecca was impressed by how Anita and Mike worked together, quietly in sync, and by their easy, unobtrusive black humor. It was a glimpse of a side of Mike she hadn't seen before. The two of them set up the IV rack beside the bed—a simple saline solution and a bag of morphine with a click mechanism to limit the dosage—in a brisk, wordless dance, and then Anita stood beside Mike while he slipped the IV needle into Phoebe's arm and connected the tubes. Rebecca hadn't realized how much of the technical part of things Mike had picked up along the way; it was clear that Anita had been training him.

Mike had also called Tom Dougherty, who showed up while they were still getting all the medical paraphernalia in place. Rebecca, who hadn't met the priest yet, had been prepared for him to some degree by Mike's wry stories, but Dougherty's fractious physical presence was still a bit of a shock. The man who had come to give the last rites to her mother looked like the guy most likely to get into a fight in an Irish bar.

"I'm sorry we have to meet this way," he said to Rebecca, after Mike had introduced them.

"We're just very grateful to you for coming so quickly, Father. It means a lot to my mother."

Dougherty shrugged as if it pained him. He actually looked furious, unsettlingly so. Mike had warned her of this as well: death pissed Dougherty off.

"Call me Tom," he said.

. . .

hile Mike, Anita, and Dougherty moved quietly around the bedroom setting things up, Rebecca went to find Mary Martha. She and Mike had already talked at the hospital about what to do with her when they got home with Phoebe. Rebecca had the sense that Mike felt Mary Martha could stay if she wanted, though he hadn't pushed it enough for her to be sure. But he hadn't disagreed when Rebecca had decided to call Rory to come get their daughter and keep her for the duration, and Rebecca had been grateful for that. It seemed to her that it was one thing for your grandmother to die but another thing entirely to be there when it happened and have that last image frozen in your brain for the rest of your life.

She found her daughter in the studio, in the big armchair that Phoebe had been using. Mary Martha had her grandmother's needlepoint-in-progress in her hands; she was clearly trying to figure how to work on it. Rebecca's heart hurt at that.

The armchair was big enough for two, and she slipped into it beside Mary Martha and put her arm around her.

"Will you teach me how to do this, if Gran-Gran can't?" Mary Martha said.

"Of course, sweetie."

"I want to finish it for her, as a surprise."

Rebecca blinked fast for a moment; she really didn't want to cry just yet. She said, "You know your grandmother is very sick now."

Mary Martha nodded somberly. "Her brain is hurt."

"Yes."

"And she's going to heaven soon."

"Did Mike tell you that?"

"Daddy did."

Rebecca digested that for a moment. Rory, as far as she knew, styled himself spiritually as some kind of Zen pagan; she suspected that he believed Phoebe's elements would merge with the life force or something or that death was actually an illusion if you smoked enough dope. But she could appreciate him keeping it simple, mythologically, for his daughter at crunch time. Nobody really wanted someone they loved to disappear into the damn life force. You wanted someplace you could meet up later.

She said, "Well, that's right, she's going to heaven very soon. And now it's time for us to say good-bye to her and tell her how much we love her."

Mary Martha nodded and looked at the needlepoint in her hands.

"Will her brain still be hurt, in heaven?" she asked.

Rebecca's eyes filled with tears afresh, and she blinked through them again. Still not time to cry. She said, "Do you remember that time at the beach, when you went into the water with Gran-Gran and the waves were too big and she lifted you up over them? And you two were laughing so much and you said she was the coolest grandmother in the world?"

Mary Martha smiled. "Yes."

"That is how she will be in heaven," Rebecca said.

•   •   •

Dougherty made short work of the last rites; with Mike quietly assisting, the ceremony had much the same flavor as the setting up of the IV lines, and it went almost as quickly. Standing with her hands on Mary Martha's shoulders, while the priest blessed each of Phoebe's extremities in turn, Rebecca looked at her mother's uncomprehending face and remembered the first time they had gone through this, on an afternoon the previous autumn, after Phoebe's first stroke. Her mother had been comatose then, and it seemed like a pretty sure thing that she wasn't going to make it. Rebecca knew Phoebe would want a priest, but the thought of calling an official stranger with a holy agenda stuck in her throat. She had been mad at the Catholic Church for decades by then for all the standard reasons, and she saw nothing in her mother's dying that inclined her to lighten up on either God or His damn institution.

Instead, she had called Mike, who was working at McDonald's then. He had come straight from work, spattered with grease and reeking of hamburger, still wearing his bright blue uniform like a clown suit and a bright yellow name tag with a picture of a grinning Ronald McDonald that said, in red, "Hi! My Name Is MIKE! You Deserve A Break Today!" They had been sleeping together less than two weeks at that point.

Mike had been reluctant at first to perform what amounted to a guerrilla sacrament and argued briefly for the letter of the canon law, but in the end he knew perfectly well that Rebecca was right, that Phoebe would have wanted it according to the spirit and not sweated the details. The jury-rigged ritual had been perfect, simple and true, at once impersonal and unnervingly intimate. Dispensing holy water from a Dixie cup and olive oil for the unction straight from the Bertolli's bottle, Mike had seemed like a timeless stranger, had disappeared somehow as Mike, like an opening door, and through the gap where he had been Rebecca had felt the warm surge of blessing, despite her rage, and the first touch of an unimaginable peace.

Dougherty was a different kind of priest, Rebecca thought now, watching him trace the final sign of the cross on Phoebe's forehead. She could feel the hard edge of his sublimated fury, like a razor in a sheath. If Mike was a flute, clear, serene, and intricate, backed by violins, Dougherty was brass and bass and a pounding drum. But the music of the sacrament was the same, and Rebecca felt again, in spite of herself and her complexities, the reality of the blessing, and of her mother's soul, poised before the mystery of a welcoming grace.

"Make speed to aid her, ye saints of God; come forth to meet her, ye angels of the Lord; receiving her soul, and presenting her before the face of the Most High...."

Mary Martha was crying now, but all the saints of God and angels of the Lord in the world weren't going to change that. There was nothing to do there but just keep loving. Rebecca took her daughter in her arms and held her, her own lips still moving with the prayer.

"Rest eternal grant unto her, O Lord; and let perpetual light shine upon her. Amen."

Rory and Chelsea showed up a few minutes later. It was starting to feel a little like one of the parties Phoebe had often thrown during the years of her widowhood at her house near Stinson Beach, eclectic affairs populated by artists, Buddhists, massage therapists, and freelance spiritual nutcases. Her mother had always drawn a heterodox crowd. Rory's eyes were already rimmed with red. He was holding Stu-J, jouncing him gently. Chelsea was carrying a still-warm casserole and some kind of fat scented candle. Rebecca recognized the casserole at once: it was macaroni and tuna fish, another of Phoebe's foolproof recipes for rookie chefs. Somehow, through everything else, her mother had found time to teach Rory's second wife to cook too.

"This is the candle we burned when my grandmother died," Chelsea said shyly. "It's lavender, hydrangea, and white lilac."

"It smells great," Rebecca said. "God knows, Phoebe loves her flowers."

"It's soy."

"What?"

"The wax," Chelsea said. "It's soy bean pod wax. It burns cleaner."

"Wow. I had no idea."

"It has a lead-free wick," Chelsea said.

Rebecca, to her own surprise, began to sob, for the first time. She really hadn't seen the tears coming. Chelsea immediately put her free arm around her and started crying too. Rory stood awkwardly to one side, still holding Stu-J and patting the two women with his free hand. With tears streaming down Rory's face too, for a while the baby was the only one not crying.

When the wave of tears had passed, Chelsea went to put the casserole away. Rebecca noted that she went straight to the living room to do it. It seemed an odd but accurate measure of the degree of unanticipated intimacy she had grown into with Rory's second wife that Chelsea took it as a matter of course that the refrigerator was in the living room.

Rebecca took Stu-J from Rory, put her nose on his forehead, and breathed him in. He smelled like lavender; maybe Chelsea had test-burned the candle or something.

"Who's that holding you, Stoojie?" Rory said. "Who's that nuzzling your head?"

Stu-J smiled his dazzling smile. "*Wuh*-behg."

"Oh, my God, he said it," Rebecca exclaimed.

"Can you doubt this child's genius?" Rory said, and, to Stu-J, "That's right, buddy. That's your Aunt Wuhbehg."

"Wuhbehg's going to eat your ear," Rebecca told Stu-J. "Grrr-ruf! Yum-yum!"

Stu-J giggled. What a giggle that kid had.

"How's Phoebe doing?" Rory said.

"She's pretty out of it," Rebecca said, feeling the tears close again, concentrating on the baby's face to keep them at bay for the moment. "The doctors said they'd be surprised if she makes it through the night. But you know Phoebe. I keep expecting her to wake up and insist on taking her afternoon walk."

"How's Mary Martha handling it?"

"She started crying during the last rites, and kept going for a while. But I think she's all right, all things considered. She's in the studio now, sitting in the Phoebe chair. She wants to finish her needlepoint for her."

"That's our girl," Rory said.

Rebecca hesitated, then said, "She said you told her Phoebe was going to heaven."

Rory looked embarrassed. "Well, yeah. Was that okay?"

"Of course," Rebecca said. "I mean, that's my story too, and I'm sticking to it. I was just surprised."

"Well, Mike and I had talked about it, you know—"

"You did?" Rebecca said, trying to picture it.

"Sure. We sort of agreed that it would probably be best to not get her all confused with conflicting mythologies. I mean, jeez, the kid's just turned eight, her grandmother's dying. She just needs something to hang onto. There will be plenty of time in the long run to give her more perspective on the cultural contingency of the, uh, hermeneutic constructs."

Rebecca laughed. "Mike didn't really say that, did he? About the hermeneutic constructs?"

Rory smiled. "Well, no, that's me, of course. And Derrida. You know Mike. I think what he actually said was that there was plenty of time to sort out the pony from the horseshit."

"Probably best to just stick with heaven for the time being," Rebecca said.

"That's what I'm thinking too."

They were silent a moment. It was strange for Rebecca to realize how sure she was that Rory would handle the responsibility of taking Mary Martha, how much she trusted him and Chelsea at this point with their daughter. She had actually come to count on him.

She said, "I really do appreciate you guys taking her."

"Oh, God, of course."

"No, it means a lot to me that she's going to be with you guys. I feel bad enough sending her away. I'm afraid maybe she'll be . . . traumatized—you know, missing out. She'll be on some therapist's couch in twenty years saying that her mother kept her away from her dying grandmother and it's warped her whole outlook on life."

"My grandmother died with a look on her face that I wish I'd never seen," Rory said. "Let's face it, if Mary Martha is not in therapy for one thing, she'll be in it for another." He gave her a grin. "She'll have been working on father issues for five years, anyway, by the time she even touches on this grandmother stuff."

Rebecca laughed, weirdly heartened by the truth of that. "I think Mike thinks she could handle it."

"Mike spent the last twenty years wearing one color and thinking about God," Rory said. "He's got an unusual perspective. Mary Martha is eight years old. Let her remember her grandmother alive."

Chelsea returned from the living room just then and smiled when she saw Rebecca holding Stu-J.

"Who's that holding you, Buster Blue Eyes?" she said. "Who's your favorite auntie?"

"Wuhbehg," Stu-J said, quite firmly this time. He seemed very pleased to have found something that would make all the grown-ups laugh.

S he could smell lavender, but maybe that was the morphine, and she was smelling something in the garden in New Jersey in 1958 or from her mother's garden when Mr. Hoover was president. There was a part of her brain that could still place everything in space and time, more or less, and know when it was misplaced. That understood there were people she loved coming and going, that there were IV lines, saline and sedatives, and everyone fretting over ponderous medical procedures that affected nothing. Phoebe thought she might still be at the hospital, or perhaps they had brought her back to Rebecca's house; she'd lost it to that extent, but that didn't matter anymore. And yet that earnest little part of her brain went on and on, trying heroically to keep it all straight. Like the navigation officer on the *Titanic,* still on duty in the tiny map cubicle with the charts and figures, still drawing the arcs on the map and making calculations based on the latest information. It didn't matter a bit, but she knew, give or take a few nautical miles, where she was going down.

The sea was everywhere now, was the thing, and always had been. Once you saw that, it was easy. This bed was the sea, and this smell of flowers; and the love of the ones she loved, and the mystery of the next moment; and soon enough the sea would enclose her. She'd thought for what now seemed like such a ridiculously long time that the sea was something you had to *get* to, but it turned out that was just the last hurrah of the navigation officer and the captain's ego. In the end, the sea came to you. Most of what you'd been doing up to that point, indeed, was keeping it away.

Bit by bit, the activity in the house settled, like a party coming to an end. Rory and Chelsea made their quiet good-byes at Phoebe's bedside and took Mary Martha home with them. Mary Martha was still clutching Phoebe's needlepoint; Chelsea had assured Rebecca she knew how to do it and would teach Mary Martha. Meanwhile, Mike and Dougherty had two beers and a few cigarettes on the back porch, and then Dougherty gave Rebecca a surprisingly sweet hug and went back to the Tenderloin to feed his guys dinner.

Anita stayed until late afternoon, making sure everything was in place and working, but in the end she gave them her cell phone number and began gathering her things to leave too. At the prospect of losing her professional presence, Rebecca finally felt her first real sense of the weight of what they had taken on and the first touch of panic. She said, embarrassed by the plaintive note, "Aren't you going to stay?"

Anita hesitated and glanced at Mike, who shrugged: cleared to tell the truth. She turned back to Rebecca and said gently, "There's really nothing I can do for her at this point that you can't do better yourselves."

Rebecca nodded. She realized that she had expected more of a hubbub, an atmosphere of crisis, extraordinary measures at the ready, skilled medical people working at the limits of their capacity. But of course that was not it. The doctors had said Phoebe might have hours or days, but they all agreed little could be done except to make her comfortable. She had brought her mother home to die. There was really not that much to it.

While Mike saw Anita out, Rebecca went back to Phoebe's side, sat down, and took her mother's hand. The late afternoon sun streaming through the window was warm on the wood floor, with dust motes floating lazily through the beam. The candle Chelsea had brought flickered quietly on the far dresser, burned down almost to the border between the top, light purple, layer, and the second, red, one. Apparently Chelsea's grandmother had died before the end of the lavender, and the delicate scent suffused the room.

Phoebe's nails were a wreck, Rebecca noted idly; they had been meaning to get them done for a while. The high, ruffled collar of the old-fashioned nightgown made Phoebe look like a child; the frozen unresponsiveness of her face made her seem like a stranger; and all the lines of her life, etched more deeply now with her face slumping, made her seem ancient, inscrutable, and sadly spent. It was hard to find the mother she knew anywhere amid it all, and Rebecca felt a second wave of terror. She really didn't think that she could handle this.

She rode past it, and when the fear had settled into something that felt manageable again, she rose, went into the bathroom, and returned in a moment with her manicure set. It was something to do at least, Rebecca thought, as she took out the emery board and gently began to work on her mother's limp left hand. Phoebe had always been a stickler for basic maintenance.

Mike returned just as she finished the glossy underlayer of enamel and began to apply the first touches of soft pink polish. He smiled when he saw what she was doing. Rebecca had expected something formal from him, somehow, some acknowledgment of the moment's weight, but all he said was, "That's a great color for her." Then he took his place without ceremony in the chair on the other side of the bed, and she had never loved him more, her husband and partner, her lover and her friend, waiting as she was for her mother to die.

The pain turned to music, and the music softened into warm rain, so gentle that once you were wet you couldn't feel it as something different than what you were. And the thirsty flowers opened and their scent became the sky. The work was done, and what there had been to give was given. The rain was time and it fell and fell, so softly and tenderly that it hit nothing, even memory, and the falling was a music without an up or down, its sound still looking for a place to touch. And this was love, and this, and what was next, the place it fell to touch, was love. And there was no next but this, and this was love, and love again, and there was no next but this but love and there was no next.

None of it was what she had expected, in the end. It was really very simple. There was only Phoebe's face, and all their love, and the window growing brighter with the sunset and then dark. The room settled into a silence so complete that all you could hear was the occasional click of the IV pump and the faint, stressed rhythm of Phoebe's breath. Rebecca took her mother's hand and held it to her lips, waiting for fear and grief, for pain and the searing consciousness of loss, but there was only Phoebe's face and all their love, and the silence deepened, until it seemed you could hear the candle, burning quietly as the lavender faded into hydrangea; and finally, as the sound of Phoebe's breathing ceased and her hand began to cool against Rebecca's lips, the hydrangea into white lilac.

Chapter Thirteen

But where shall wisdom be found?
And where is the place of understanding?
Man knoweth not the price thereof;
neither is it found in the land of the living.

JOB 28:12–13

The sand at Ocean Beach was warm for once in an unimpeded summer sun, and the rare onshore breeze was blessedly mild. Many of the mourners had arrived dressed in cautious sweatshirts and jackets, a nod to the vagaries of the Bay Area's climate, but as the miracle of the weather persisted, everyone stripped down to shorts and T-shirts and even the occasional bathing suit. The surf was up from a storm somewhere out in the Pacific, and the surfers in the crowd, including Rory, bobbed on the sparkling water beyond the breakers in a stolid line of patient silhouettes, like an honor guard in wet suits. No one had really planned the food, and they'd been troubled by the prospect of an unrelieved avalanche of potato chips, but there was a loaves-and-fishes thing happening, with rickety card tables sagging with potato salad and casseroles and three-bean salads and all manner of unidentifiable greenery, and half a dozen barbecue grills filling the air with the smell of everything from hamburgers and hot dogs to chicken, teriyaki tofu, and grilled stuffed peppers. It was way too much food, indeed, a mad amount of food, and they'd already made arrangements to take the leftovers to St. Luke's Mission. There were also dozens of teeming coolers, kegs, and wine of every description and provenance, but that seemed less miraculous: there had never been any doubt this crowd would have the alcohol covered.

Sitting on a blanket, listening to the reggae band play "One Love" and watching Mary Martha and Mike filling big red balloons with helium and tying them to people's wrists, Rebecca could only shake her head in astonishment. She'd been inclined all along to write off Phoebe's preposterous notion of a come-as-you-are, BYOB, potluck funeral as a side effect of dementia. She had humored her mother, and Mike, when they had talked about it like gleeful coconspirators, but she had figured that when the time came they would all have been sobered sufficiently by the reality of death to just have a basic wake like her father's, a dim room full of people wearing dark clothes, powering somberly through the litany of the rosary and exchanging condolences in hushed voices; and then a good grim funeral mass with some priest who'd never known Phoebe trying to pretend that the eventual resurrection of the dead could be any comfort at all. But it was obvious to Rebecca now that her mother's sense of social felicity had been unerring as always. The people who would have come to a wake and funeral mass were all on the East Coast and had sent flowers, or were dead themselves. Phoebe's West Coast friends, the exotic fruit of her unruly widowhood, would celebrate her passing to the music of a different drummer, with a reggae beat.

People kept stopping by the blanket to tell her their favorite Phoebe stories. It was amazing what death set loose, as if a flock of birds, scattered invisibly through a grove of trees, had been startled into the air all at once in a flurry of winged moments: acts of secret mercy and philanthropy, wit and wildness, friendship and wisdom, flushed from every direction to darken the sky in a sudden coherence. Rebecca hadn't stopped crying for more than five minutes at a time since she'd gotten here. But it seemed like that was part of her job today.

A Frisbee hit the sand beside her, followed a moment later by Bruiser, Bonnie's German shepherd, in an explosion of sand, and then by Rory's Labrador, Bruno. Both dogs had red balloons tied to their collars, which only complicated the mayhem. The two dogs scuffled briefly, sand flying everywhere, before Bruiser got a good grip on the Frisbee and took off with Bruno on his heels.

Bonnie, out of breath, arrived just as the dogs moved on and Rebecca began brushing herself off.

"Sorry about that," she said. "Bob's a little wild today."

"No problem," Rebecca said.

"Are you okay?"

"Dehydrated from crying. But basically fine."

Bonnie paused, trying to gauge her actual condition, then said, apparently deciding to roll with it, "You want me to grab you a beer? Keep up your fluid intake?"

Rebecca held up her drink, indicating that she was fine. Bonnie did a double take at the Diet Coke, and then gave her a sly grin.

"Okay," she said. "Either you're on the wagon, orrrr ... "

"You have a dirty mind, young lady," Rebecca said. "I'm just counting calories. I've been eating nothing but Good Samaritan casseroles for a week."

"Grief is fattening," Bonnie conceded. "I gained ten pounds when my grandmother died."

"Bonnie!" Bob called. "You still playing?"

"You go ahead," Bonnie hollered back. "I'm going to hang here for a while." She sat down beside Rebecca on the blanket. "What a bash, huh?"

"Mom always drew an interesting crowd."

"It's so weird that she's not here. I keep expecting to see her, pouring the wine or something. Serving those little things she used to make—"

"The tea sandwiches?"

"Yeah. Horseradish salmon cream and asparagus."

"Chicken salad with cream cheese and pecans."

"And those ones with the sun-dried tomatoes and bacon. On that silver tray."

"Phoebe was the only woman I ever knew who could say arugula and havarti in the same sentence without smirking," Rebecca said.

"Arugula with a straight face," Bonnie agreed. "Now *that's* a legacy."

Chelsea approached them just then, carrying Stu-J and three red balloons, and sat down on Rebecca's right.

"What an awesome party," she said. "Phoebe would have loved this."

"I wouldn't have bet a dime it would come off right," Rebecca said.

"How are *you* doing?"

"I'm missing the tea sandwiches," Rebecca said. "But basically okay." She bent toward Stu-J. "Arugula, kiddo! Arugula! Arugula!"

"Wuhbehg!"

"Havarti! Havarti, Stu-J!"

"Wuhbehg!"

"You guys have got to see this," Chelsea said. She lifted Stu-J and set him upright on the sand in front of them, held him briefly under the arms, then let him go. He wobbled for an instant, with a slightly alarmed look on his face, then settled into his stance and gave them his grin.

"Oh, my God," Bonnie said. "He's upright! Stu-J, you're a biped!"

"Bed," Stu-J seconded proudly.

"He's got Rory's sense of balance," Rebecca said. "He'll be hanging five in no time."

"Rory actually wants to get him a little surfboard," Chelsea said, and, as Stu-J lost it and plopped back on his diapered butt, "I wish Phoebe could have seen this."

"And his first step, and his high school graduation," Rebecca agreed. She thought she might cry again, but she reached out and set Stu-J upright again instead, then sipped her Diet Coke. She actually *was* pregnant, she was pretty sure, the stick had turned pink twice, but she didn't really see how she could tell Bonnie or Chelsea before she figured out how in the world she was going to tell Mike.

There were only so many ways you could say how much Phoebe would have loved the party, and after several more of them Bonnie and Chelsea settled into an earnest discussion of prenatal development and the pros and cons of midwives. Mary Martha finally determined that everyone had enough red balloons, and she ran off to play with Bob and the dogs. The band took a short break and then began playing a series of songs that people had written especially for Phoebe. Rebecca cried at the first two, but the series threatened to go on and she was relieved when Mike finally worked his way over to the blanket, assessed her condition at a glance, and suggested that they take a walk. She was pretty much cried out by now, and her head felt like it might explode from all the caffeine and grief. She hadn't foreseen how grueling it would be to act as the emotional lightning rod for all of Phoebe's friends.

They walked toward the rocks at the end of the beach, holding hands. They had just cleared the main body of the party when they spotted the policeman coming toward them from the board-walk.

"Shit," Rebecca said. "Now it turns into a *real* Phoebe party."

"It will be okay," Mike said. "We'll throw ourselves on the mercy of the human being inside the uniform."

"You are a truly naive man, darling. You can smell the dope from here."

"Maybe the wind will shift."

"Is there a problem, officer?" Rebecca said as the man reached them. He was maybe thirty, clean-cut and earnest. His name tag read PERKINS, and he looked genuinely unhappy about his job, but not unhappy enough.

"I hate to be a party pooper, but I'm afraid those dogs running around are in violation of the leash law."

"I'm sorry. We didn't realize."

"Probably the six-inch letters on the sign aren't big enough," Perkins agreed. "Do you all have a permit for that band?"

"You need a permit?"

"And I don't know how to tell you this, ma'am, but I suspect that there is alcohol being consumed here."

"It's a funeral," Rebecca said, deciding to try Mike's approach.

The policeman laughed. "Yeah, right."

"No, really. Well, a memorial service. For my mother."

Perkins gave her a sharp glance and realized she was serious. He hesitated a moment, then said, "I'm sorry for your loss, ma'am. I truly am. But—"

"Could we offer you a bribe of some sort?" Mike said.

The cop looked at him coldly. Mike met his eyes with his usual air of saintly mildness, and the whole thing hung for a long moment on the man's sense of humor.

Finally Perkins shook his head.

"What was your mother's name?" he asked Rebecca.

"Phoebe. Phoebe Marie Martin."

"I lost my mom last year," Perkins said. "I have a border collie, I happen to like reggae, and I've been known to imbibe the occasional beer. But I'm going to come back here in half an hour, and if I can still smell marijuana from the boardwalk, I'm going to come down here and kick ass and take names. Fair enough?"

"More than fair," Rebecca said. "Thank you, Officer."

"God bless your mother," Perkins said. "She was obviously very much loved. May she rest in peace."

He turned and walked back up toward his car. They watched until he was gone, and then Rebecca looked at Mike and said, "Did you learn that in the monastery, about trying to bribe policemen, or is that just something you picked up since you started teaching Sunday school?"

"I'm just glad he didn't go for it," Mike said. "I've only got five bucks."

They paused to relay the policeman's ultimatum, and a perceptible ripple ran through the crowd as those so inclined hastened to get in their last tokes. Rebecca hoped Perkins didn't come back early, or half the crowd at her mother's funeral would end up in jail.

She and Mike walked on, leaving the party behind for the second time and managing this time to get clear. It was amazing how quickly it got quiet as you moved away. No doubt that was partly because the band was taking a hasty break to join the general last-minute run on the available intoxicants. But there was also the deep and simple comfort of Mike's undemanding silence, the sense that words were not necessary between them at this point, and the sudden and fresh realization of the healing expanse of sand, sky, and sea, beyond the hothouse emotions of the memorial scene. It was a relief to Rebecca to finally be somewhere where the next thing said to her would not necessarily require her to cry.

They threaded their way through the beginning of the rocks at the base of the Cliff House, until they found a flat spot on a big boulder in the sun that felt private. From here, Phoebe's memorial celebration looked like a convention of red balloons.

"It reminds me of our wedding," Rebecca said. "Sitting on the rock by that hut of yours."

"Me too."

"Is that weird?"

"Completely," Mike said. "But no weirder than anything else, really."

"That was the last party Phoebe planned."

"That one was a bit much too, as I recall."

Rebecca laughed. That was her man. "I was actually afraid you were going to bolt, that day."

"No way. I was a goner."

"That's what Phoebe said, then."

"She always had my number," Mike said. "It helped that you brought the champagne, though."

They were silent for a time, holding hands. The tide was still coming in, and the first wave touched the base of the rock on which they sat. Rebecca thought of the brand-new boulder on the beach near Kilauea in Hawaii, its molten stone just hardening, turning the waves to steam until it cooled. She had thought that new rock was like their marriage then, an incandescent, still-forming gift from the incomprehensible fire at the heart of the earth; and, like their marriage, this rock they sat on now had long since cooled to surface temperature and found its basic shape. But it was lovely, to be able to sit here like this in the sun. You couldn't do that on fresh-dripped lava.

Mike said, "I couldn't help but notice that you're drinking Coke today."

Rebecca met his eyes and saw at once that he knew. She wondered when he'd figured it out. It was like him, to have waited to bring it up until it seemed like a relief that he had.

She said, "Are you … okay, with that?"

"I have nothing whatsoever against Coke," he said. "It's the real thing. Things go better with it."

"There's still time to bolt, you know."

There was a stir on the beach off to their left; the milling masses of the party were acquiring a kind of coherence. Sherilou, the high priestess of a coven Phoebe had befriended along the way, was marshaling everyone into some kind of spiral dance, with a consequent confusion of balloons. It was time, clearly, for the Spiritual part.

"I ran out of places to bolt, when I met you," Mike said.

Chapter Fourteen

I am convinced that neither death, nor life,
nor angels, nor kings, nor things present, nor things to come,
nor powers, nor heights, nor depths,
will be able to separate us from the love of God.

ROMANS 8:38–39

By the time they got back, the spiral dance had run its course, the balloons had been untangled, and people were gathering along the edge of the water. Sherilou, her ceremonial blue gown hanging a little heavily on her now, soaked at the hem by a surprise wave, was issuing some final, crucial spiritual instructions, wisdom and insight, mercifully inaudible over the roar of the surf. The surfers had all come ashore except Rory, who sat placidly on his board beyond the breakers, holding the urn with Phoebe's ashes in it. Rebecca met Mike's eyes, and he smiled quietly. She knew they were thinking the same thing. Her mother had made it to the sea at last.

As they took their place in the crowd, Mary Martha ran over to them, her face pink with sun and still alight from the fun of the dance. She'd been drinking Coke too, Rebecca recognized, and there was going to be hell to pay at bedtime. But at least the kid was having fun at her grandmother's funeral. She could recall her own grandfather's wake and funeral; it still felt heavy in her stomach, like an undercooked dumpling. The vision of all the main grown-ups in her world in tears had been completely unnerving to her at age six, and she'd found comfort only in the spectacle of her grandfather's cronies solemn and inscrutable in their Knights of Columbus uniforms, complete with swords. She had actually never seen Pop-Pop in his admiral's outfit until he lay in his coffin, and it had given her one of her first glimpses of unsuspected realms of deep and exotic meaning in the lives of her familiar adults.

Mary Martha planted herself precisely between the two of them, cuddling up against their bodies, and Rebecca and Mike each put a hand on one of her shoulders. Bonnie and Bob came over too, with Bruiser, and then Chelsea, looking a little over-whelmed with both Bruno on his leash and Stu-J in her arms. Mike took Stu-J from her and hoisted the toddler up so that he could see. Rebecca hadn't had a chance yet, with all the flurry, to tell Rory and Chelsea that Phoebe had remembered them some-what spectacularly in her will. Stu-J had a college fund now.

The band kicked into a reggae-beat cover of "Knocking on Heaven's Door." It was supposed to be instrumental, but when the first chorus came around, everyone began to sing the lyrics anyway, spontaneously, and Rebecca's arms tightened into goose-flesh. She had to smile at that. Her mother's parties always man-

aged a moment like this somehow, when all the things that more
or less just gave Rebecca a headache had run their course and the
holiness slipped in somehow, as if in spite of all their best efforts.

Rory sat on his board, turned sideways to the shore, waiting
for his wave. He let several go by that seemed perfectly fine to
Rebecca, but that was Rory. She remembered her mother's first
visit after Rory and Rebecca had gotten together. They had gone
to the beach the first day, inevitably, and Phoebe and Rebecca
had sat on a blanket while Rory surfed. It had been a slow day
and Rory had spent hours just sitting out there, heedless and
patient as a channel marker. Rebecca had been painfully con-
scious of what she feared her mother would take to be rudeness
on her new boyfriend's part, but at twenty-three she had been
disinclined to make excuses for anything, and she had just let
Phoebe make of Rory what she would. And so she and Phoebe
had chatted, and shivered in the thin sun, and finally wrapped
blankets around themselves; and still Rory had sat quietly waiting,
until it had gone on so long that Rebecca couldn't stand it anymore, and said to Phoebe apologetically, "He really isn't doing
this to be perverse."

"You can't force the ocean," Phoebe had said placidly. "But
thank God we brought wine."

The first chorus ended, and the band settled into a lilting,
unhurried jam. The crowd fell silent, a congregation of bobbing
red balloons, straining slightly seaward with the mild onshore
breeze. Back on the boardwalk, Rebecca saw that Officer Perkins
had returned, right on schedule. He stood at the top of the steps,

having apparently found the air sufficiently clear to let them be. He had taken off his hat, she noted.

Rory bobbed over another set of swells. Sherilou was trying to signal him to move things along, as if he'd missed a cue. Good luck, girl, Rebecca thought. But no one else was in a hurry at this point; and meanwhile, the hush of the waiting crowd was so sweet. It made Rebecca think of the quiet of the candlelit room through Phoebe's last hours: a silence of fullness, edged with ache. She had known grief only as a kind of rage, and furious bafflement; it came easily to her that way. Or as despair, as something that ravaged, and as a defeat. But this was a grief of peace, slow and strong and sure and deep. It was like the quiet she felt in Mike's arms, and the moment before the next brushstroke, and all the surprises of quiet in all the humblings of parenthood and friendship, the moments that flanked the tumult and stalemate of what you'd thought you knew and slipped free into fields of stillness. She couldn't even say anymore where it had begun, whether in love or loss, in beauty or in pain. But it was there all the time now; she had only to stop for a moment to become aware of it, like earth or sky or the beat of her own heart. It was very strange, Rebecca thought, she really hadn't seen it coming, but the emotion she had felt most deeply, in these raw days after her mother's death, was gratitude.

A fresh set of waves came in, and Rory let one pass, and another, then turned to catch the third. He paddled hard, the urn between his knees, and came to his feet in one swift motion. The wave was breaking right to left, and as the swell gathered and began to curl he turned straight back up toward the crest and then cut sharply back and settled in to the ride, cleaving a glass-cutter's line along the smooth inner face of the curl, just ahead of the breaking edge. He had the urn in his hands now, the top gone; he lifted the container, and suddenly there was a thread of gray streaming behind him, like smoke from a hidden flame.

Mary Martha's balloon slipped from her hand, dipped once in a gust of wind toward the breakers, then soared above the waves. Rebecca, who'd seen her daughter cry for hours at lost balloons before, said quickly, the awe of the moment trumped by motherhood, "It's okay, sweetie. We'll get you another one."

"You can have mine," Mike said.

"I did it on *purpose,* sillies," Mary Martha said.

Rebecca looked at Mike, who met her eyes and gave her a wry, that's-our-girl smile. The two of them let go of their own balloons at the same instant. Chelsea, always quick on the uptake, promptly released hers too, and then Bonnie, and Bob; and suddenly the air was peppered with red balloons, a gently swirling cloud, drifting toward and then above Rory and into the sky over the sea, as he worked the wave with Phoebe's urn held high, still trailing that mystery, that sifting, almost weight-less whisper of ash.

Acknowledgments

I am grateful to Gideon Weil, my gifted editor at HarperSanFrancisco, for his deftness and grace, his patience and humor, and the great joy of his friendship. I am blessed with a brilliant publishing team at HarperSF, and my deep thanks go to Mark Tauber, Michael Maudlin, Claudia Boutote, Cindy DiTiberio, Sam Barry, and all the rest of that marvelous crew. My production schedule has been eerily synced with Carolyn Allison-Holland's for quite some time, and I am grateful for her mothering my works through the process. Priscilla Stuckey's scrupulous eye and ear have kept me honest, as always, and Krista Holmstead has exercised infinite patience with me, and done a wonderful job for my work despite my best efforts to thwart her. And to Matthew Snyder, of CAA, all my thanks.

Thanks to Renée Sedliar, my editor for life, who gave the blessing of her astuteness and attention when it was most needed. I will always be grateful to Margery Buchanan and Miki Terasawa for their sustaining friendship. Jennifer Ashley's humor, camaraderie, and good writing sense remain crucial. I am grateful to, and for, Andrea Marks, for all her gifts.

Thanks to Claire and Art Poole, and to Kate Johnson, for their friendship, and for so generously keeping me afloat at the crucial moments. Sarah Moore remains a mainstay of my sanity; and my deep gratitude, always to Marilou Kollar, and my blessings for sharing her mother's beautiful example. The inspiration of Sabrina Waide, my beloved goddaughter, will always fire my heart; may I dance at her wedding, and may she sing at my funeral. My love and gratitude to the Waide family, to the Diamonds and Springers, and the Markses, to all my church community, and to my precious family. And God bless, you, Annie Poole.

Thanks, as ever, to Linda Chester, of Linda Chester Literary Agency, for unfailing kindness and the enduring comfort of elegance. And to my agent, sister novelist, and true comrade, Laurie Fox, to whom this book is dedicated and without whom it wouldn't have survived, my profound gratitude and love, for the gifts and graces of two decades of sharing the journey.

5/07